Geoffrey Heptonstall

Heaven's Invention

ISBN 978-1-911424-12-3
SKU/ID 9781911424123

Cover design by Wolf
Book design by Wolf
Editor: Monica Turoni

Publishing Company:
Black Wolf Edition & Publishing Ltd.
2 Glebe Place, Burntisland KY3 0ES, Scotland www.blackwolfedition.com

'There is no marriage in Heaven, but there is love.'
Edgar Lee Masters

One:

Guiding the Spider

6

One

I could pretend it was a dream.

Spiders move with the light. They are confused by shadows. If they move at night it is when light can guide them. Perhaps a candle burns, or there is a moon, or the streetlamps are bright. Spiders are very sensitive to sound. They hear much that they cannot see. The world of the spider does not resemble our world. They hardly know us except as the vague, menacing presence that unaccountably breaks their delicate webs and their fragile lives.

I did not see the web until it was broken when I opened the door of the summerhouse. It was quite late and very dark. There must have been a spider close by, but I saw nothing. Of course I saw nothing, neither then nor later when I returned to the house. I did not think my presence had been noted.

In the apartment I made sure that everything was secure for the night before we slept. There ought to have been a clock in the distance sounding the hour, but we could hear nothing except perhaps the distant hum of those voices down below us in Paradise Park. If there were other sounds we were so accustomed to them they did not register. Even the noise from the park was barely there. Bath was not a large city. It slept quite early. Revellers by this time had made their way home.

Caroline closed the shutters leading onto the balcony we rarely used. Where the air had been refreshingly cool now it was simply cold, for the time was late and the evening had turned into night. We looked back at the room filled with all that our friends had left behind, and we knew we were finished, Caroline and I at the end of a successful party. There was nothing more to be done until the morning.

On the balcony we had watched the lights of the city flash with the swaying of the trees below us. There was a hint of a mist, or smoke from fires in the park perhaps.

When it is dark, when something takes place that is the dark. When it is out of sight, and silent, we can pretend to ourselves that it's not really happening. It is a dream we are having.

'Dave was so funny,' I said.

'Good old Dave,' Caroline agreed. She was relaxed now. 'He always brings matters down to earth.'

Dave Marsh was our neighbour and our friend. We had little in common except that we were neighbours. But Dave was an amiable, helpful man. He was also an opinionated bigot and a drunken fool whose wife had left him bereft of any understanding of life when she walked out without a word one Sunday afternoon as he was dozing on the couch in front of the football. 'Such an odd thing to do,' was all he could find say. 'Of course, you know, there was instability in that family. It comes out. Thank God the kids take after me. Not that I see them much now.'

'Yes, it stopped me from feeling upset, talking to Dave.' I drank more wine. Caroline surprised me by taking more wine after cognac. She was no longer sober. Drink had lulled her suspicions as much as anything I had done to disarm her. I had to explain my long absence earlier in the summerhouse. It was a relief to see her mellowing in the glow of a successful evening.

'We're lucky to have such friends,' Caroline said. It was true. We were lucky in our friends. I thought at once of Rosaline, my partner in business, and Jane, her partner in life. Through our work we had met so many people whom we saw as friends as well as colleagues and customers.

'Even Dave,' I said. Yes, even Dave Marsh. For all his faults we were lucky to know him if only because he was useful to us in the contacts he knew. But more than that, for all his faults he was an interesting man, well-meaning, generous and (often not intentionally) amusing.

'Oh, he's a good man at heart,' Caroline said, echoing my thoughts. 'It's the innocence I like. I mean, he just doesn't know anything. He can't see himself. He's probably a lot happier for that.'

I tried not to think of the summerhouse where I had found Ruth alone. We barely spoke before we embraced with that edge of danger. It was wrong to cross a certain boundary even by a few steps. I reached out to her, lightly touching her hips, when Ruth withdrew, again without a word. That was the end of the incident. Had we been witnessed even that would have compromised us so severely. But no-one came near the summerhouse - as far as we knew. Nothing was seen as far as we knew. Nothing was known before it was over. It never happened. Surely, it never happened?

I could say more or less truthfully that I didn't speak to Ruth in the garden. But that was as far as the truth went. I had lied to avoid hurt to Caroline. More to the point, I had lied to avoid hurt to myself. An admission would have created a tension that could never be resolved entirely.

I had never betrayed Caroline before. But I had been tempted. Ruth had nothing that Caroline didn't have. It was the variation that interested me. There were similar, as friends often are, but not similar in the way sisters are. Had I not loved Caroline I might have loved Ruth.

The thought of being with both of them, though not at the same time, had drifted into my mind: Caroline, the lovely, dependable wife: Ruth, the lonely divorcee in search of love. It has been known to happen.

'Good old Dave,' I echoed, not really caring about Dave Marsh at this time. I hoped my tone was not cynical. 'He is a good man at heart,' I added.

'You're not entirely sure, are you?'

'Well, he can be annoying. I mean…'

'I know his faults. And I know he really does mean well. He's a good neighbour. He has been helpful. We know he'd be there if we needed him.'

'Yes,' I said, 'that's something. We're lucky.'

Then there was nothing to be said. I thought I heard something outside in the garden, supposing it to be some nocturnal creature. More happens in the dark of night than we like to think. We talk of peace when the truth is that things are happening.

Caroline yawned, got up from the couch, and put her empty glass on the table, making her way to the door. She paused, looking down. On the floor there was something I could not make out. Caroline picked it up. 'Someone's ear ring,' she said. 'I wonder whose?'

'Maybe we'll find out.'

'Come up when you're ready,' Caroline said, making her way upstairs.

I ought never to have gone into the garden that night. Then my life should have been different. That is to say it should have been the same. We can't predict anything for certain. There are always likelihoods.

It was likely that Caroline and I would go on living for a while in this place. But the fact was that earlier I had gone down to the garden, and I entered a different world. Opening the summerhouse I broke the delicate thread between one life and another. In the morning I thought the garden would be the same, and that I should be the same. That is what I hoped, even as I knew that the world had changed as I slept. Something was working its way into my life.

Geoffrey Heptonstall

Two

We lived in an intimate city. At times it seemed to have the intimacy of a village. It was not a place where one could remain anonymous for long. People became known.

Of course there were those who drifted through, perhaps lingering for a summer before moving on who knows where. But anyone who established roots was likely to become well known, if only at a distance. Strangers soon were people you recognized. Even if you never spoke to them they were people you knew by sight. Something of their lives revealed itself when they passed by in the street.

Because it was a genteel English city it was a haven for the elderly, lonely poor whose poverty had not diminished their gentility. They tried to keep up appearances in well-worn clothes, in small furnished rooms. They lived no doubt on the inevitably saddening remembrance of past achievements. And they lived on future hopes that were never going to be realized. *This was not how things really are. This is only a temporary difficulty until things are sorted out, as surely they shall be.* Coming from good families, they felt sure of resolution. One day there would be a letter from the family solicitor. It was simply a matter of waiting until things sorted themselves out.

Bath was also a haven for artists, musicians and writers, all at various stages of development. Here was an atmosphere conducive to creativity, or so it was felt. The tranquillity of the antique and the decorative attracted many in search of ways to express themselves. Galleries, performance spaces and bookshops came and went, each one gathering creative-looking people and their hangers-on. As commercial ventures they were rarely successful enough to last, but in their place would come another venture brightly-painted, energized by optimism, and peopled by charming people who had no money to buy what was on offer.

And what was that? The promise was freedom and self-fulfilment. When we looked down at Paradise Park we saw how that promise was shaping up to reality.

The reality was a city park, one of several in this elegant spa city. This one had been taken over by a group of idealists camped in a corner for a summer, then a winter. They had survived the chill mists of October, the frosts of November and December, the snows of January and the rains of February. And now it seemed that they were to remain for another summer. There was much angry talk of removing them. But the Paradise People had their liberal defenders who had kept the hounds at bay. It seemed there was no law against their presence in the park. They had committed no offence. It was going to take a court injunction to remove them. So far no writ had been served. There were rumours because there are always rumours. But thus far – it was May now – nothing had happened this year.

We lived in a house on the steep cliff overlooking the park. It was a large, old house divided into expensive apartments. People lived here for the commanding views of the city. The prospect from the top floor was impressive. We had taken the garden flat because we wanted use of the garden, although it was not ours exclusively.

We also wanted a sense of fulfilment. We had worked hard toward that end, sacrificing time and freedom so that we might buy future time and a guaranteed freedom. We were working for something quite definite, not drifting in vague hope.

When the shutters were opened the light of the morning streamed in, and I wanted to forget about the night. I heard someone moving about the garden in the morning. Looking out of the window, I saw a figure in the pale light. The figure dodged into the bushes, so I only caught a glimpse of someone I took to be an intruder. Dressing quickly, I went down to the garden. From the kitchen window I saw a slim young man walking towards the house.

Knowing he had been seen, he had decided to let himself be known. Others would have run. Almost anyone else would have run, but the young man openly and confidently walked towards the kitchen door. When I opened the door I was greeted with a disarming smile. It was as if the youth in the garden was trying to make me, the occupier, feel like an intruder.

He was not much above twenty, not many years older than I, but every year is a long time when you are young. He had a potentially handsome face, although it had yet to acquire the sense of character that comes with experience. It was a boy's face with the expression of someone schooled in privilege. The ragged look of his clothes could not disguise the commanding presence of his manner. He was rebelling against the life which inescapably defined him. 'Hi, I'm Simpson,' he said, offering his hand. His handshake was confident. So, too, was the look his eyes gave mine. 'I hope you don't mind, but I was curious to see what happened above the park.'

There was a measured charm about him, like a diplomat perhaps. There was also a sense of natural command, like an army officer. He knew how to gain advantage in situations where he had none. He knew how to invite himself into our garden, and to make himself feel welcome. 'I'm sorry if you feel...' he began, letting the rest of the sentence trail away. 'It's such a lovely garden,' Simpson added. 'I love gardens. That's why I'm here.'

'Look, I...'

'Thoughts,' he continued curtailing my protest, 'should be like migrating birds. Cage one and it turns in the direction it should be flying. If it can't fly across a continent it will do so in its dreams. No-one is quite sure how birds know where to fly. They navigate by the sun and stars, of course but they seem to follow a line we can't see. We could see it if we had the mind to. That's where I want my thinking to go.'

'So you've begun your journey?' I said, intrigued a little, and wondering if that was wise.

'This is part of it. I knew down there in the park this was the right place to be. I can be here because I feel your acceptance. More than kind, even. I see goodness in you that maybe you don't recognise. And very likely that's the reason I'm here.

'I found a garden. I see a lot happening here. This conversation, for example. I think it's important the connection we've made, you and I. I've made you think. You were a tree in full leaf. Now you've been shaken by the first winds of the fall. Or is it spring? Are you shedding leaves before winter, or blossom before the summer fruit ripens? I've made you think. I've given you choice. You didn't know you had a choice, did you? Just seeing me has made you wonder.'

'Not quite,' I replied. 'I think your rebellion is familiar enough.'

Simpson paused for a moment as he looked about the room. 'There's always something beyond,' he said. 'Like here there's the garden, then there's this house. It doesn't stop there. There's something beyond the house. Maybe another house.' He seemed to be very still, although he spoke of a restlessness. He had wandered from home, perhaps a long way. He intended to go on. I could tell that in time he would go on. This was only a step in the journey.

Simpson put his finger into the space between two stones on the kitchen wall. 'It needs attention,' he said. 'Look, this is coming loose. You can hardly see it now, but give it a few years and it will be in serious trouble.' His finger traced a line along the stones. He was pointing out what we had suspected before but dared not think. Our home needed some structural repairs. It needed to be saved from eventual collapse.

Simpson's hands felt the stones with a care of a mason. He seemed to be establishing a relationship with the stones. It was as if he had announced his intention remain in the house, and to look after it. 'It's such good stone,' he said. He was looking at the stone, not at me. I, the occupier of this place, had been dismissed as if I no longer had a right to be there.

I wanted to say, 'This is my home, so if you wouldn't mind.' I wanted to open the door and usher this interloper out, out of the house, the garden and my world. I didn't want to see him again. Let him go back to Paradise Park, or onward to wherever he might drift. What mattered was that I could continue my Sunday morning as I spent most other Sunday mornings.

'I found a garden,' Simpson said. 'And I also found this,' holding in his hand an ear ring. Ruth's other ear ring. 'In the summerhouse,' he added. 'I kept a lookout in the garden a long time.'

Simpson began to hum. At first I could not believe he was humming. I supposed the sound to be a wasplike creature perhaps. The humming grew louder as he rested the palms of his hands on the stonework. Gradually it developed into a chant, a vibratory, rhythmic evocation of mysteries – or so it seemed – of which I could not be part. I no longer mattered. I no longer existed. What was real was the stonework. It was alive with possibilities.

When he had finished Simpson turned to me, and said, 'It was the sound of sound. I like to feel in harmony with each a new situation. I was searching for the rhythm of the stones. I didn't make the sound. It was something I discovered. The sound made the sound.' Before I could reply he continued, 'It doesn't have to mean anything. What does a flower mean? Or a tree? They mean everything. They're why we're here. We're here on earth because of the living matter which could generate life and then sustain it. We need to speak to that nature which is our creation. That's why we're here.'

'Look, it's not that I don't acc...' I tried to be insistent without losing my cool. But Simpson was well-versed in the art of making people listen. I found I could not break off this conversation without feeling boorish.

'Can't you feel the enchantment? It's good to be natural. Let the world run wild. I do believe in following our natural impulses. Not every impulse, or it would be chaos. It's a question of trusting to your intuition. That must be what led me here. I could have remained where I was down in the park. We might never have met. That's an opportunity for both of us which might easily have been missed. I do like meeting intelligent people.'

There was another pause when he and I looked at each other. His eyes challenged, of course. It was a contest I knew I was losing. This strange intruder's will was stronger mine, had I dared to admit it.

'Is that the sun or the moon? No, I think it's the embers of the old world before it sinks into perpetual night. Imagine living in eternal dream-filled sleep.

That's the choice so many have made. And they think they are free. The first step to freedom is realizing your captivity.'

'I really am not sure what to make of you, Simpson. But I suppose your youth is your charm. For heaven's sake don't grow old.' That was all I could think to say. I could hear the sounds of Caroline stirring from her sleep above. She was going to be surprised.

'Growing old,' Simpson said reflectively, 'That's one thing I hope to avoid. Not death that I can't avoid. But the inner decay, the withering of spirit. That must never happen. To keep moving is the way. Imagine me becoming a statue in your garden. Well, you know what I mean.'

I wanted to say something that might have silenced Simpson into thinking. He was someone who always had an answer. And he was evidently one of those people who wanted the last word. I was determined to better him.

Before I was able to speak Caroline came down. She looked not nearly as surprised as I had imagined. 'I heard voices,' she said calmly, seeing the two of us together in the kitchen finishing our coffee. Looking back, I see now that she may have supposed Simpson to be one of the new people moving into the empty apartment. Even allowing for this, her response was calm. Of course memory filters everything, but what I recall is her matter-of-fact greeting to Simpson, as if his arrival was half expected.

Three

One evening Dave Marsh called in to see us, as he often did.

When he called that midweek evening it was to tell us he had found a new gardener, a young man who believed in gardens as an ideal space, so Marsh said. A very intelligent young man whose approach was commendable. Marsh had every faith in him. For the past few nights Simpson had been staying with Marsh, but was to be given somewhere to live for the summer. He was going to clear out the summerhouse so that he might make it habitable. Marsh assured us that the young man was very reliable and trustworthy. Surely we had no objections. Simpson was going to live in the garden.

Caroline received the news better than I did. She had found Simpson not only intriguing and charming but thoughtful and mature beyond his years. 'He'll go places,' Caroline said of him after he had collected his canvas bag and made his departure. I thought he would wander. Neither of us envisaged him getting to know Dave Marsh. Quite how it happened I never knew. He found a way into Marsh's favour, and there he took root. It was a surprise for us and possibly for Dave Marsh.

Dave Marsh had made a lot of money. He had made a lot of money in property. These were times when it was possible with both a certain amount of capital and a capacity for taking risks a speculator could be lucky.

Some weren't. Dave Marsh was lucky. He had a gift for making friends. That seemed to be his secret in making money. At the golf course, at the wine bar, at the country club Dave Marsh found business to be a pleasure. He found that with a generous smile and a generous account he could make his way into the life he enjoyed. Others had more money, but few had more influence than Marsh.

A career in politics was inevitable. He had yet to see himself as a player on the national stage. In our local world he had influence and authority. Marsh sat on several committees. He was able to ease, or to block, the path of ambitious people. It had done neither Caroline nor I harm to be on good terms with our neighbour, although we had never cultivated him for that reason alone.

His intuition was that money is nothing without an attitude that understands its limitations. Dave Marsh never sought to buy friendship or even popularity. He sought the status he had achieved by the gifts of his personality. Wealth was simply the instrument by which he could present himself.

His secret was to seemingly take you into his confidence. The hush of his tone, the intensity of his manner, the lowered head and the forward lean of his body: he spoke to you as if he trusted you.

'I think that young man has got his head screwed on. He'll go places,' he said of Simpson. 'The young... well, they drift about, don't they. The park has been of great concern to me as Deputy Chair of the Environment Committee. There's a health and safety issue that I feel is not being properly addressed. In that respect Simpson has been of great help. We need to build up a case, you see. I can't tell you how useful inside detailed information is going to be in our fight to restore some sanity to the situation.'

Caroline poured a generous measure of scotch for Marsh, for we had our measure of the man. It was a question of giving him drink, allowing him to make his speech, then to ask him questions of the matters concerning us....

All day from eight in the morning and well into the evening Simpson worked in the summerhouse. He was clearing it of all its contents. Items to be discarded were arranged in neat piles on the lawn. In the afternoon a builder's skip arrived. Men in orange overalls loaded the garbage into the skip. The surprise was how much there was to be taken away: an old, damp carpet, rotting wooden chairs, rusting garden implements, piles of newspapers, cushions, boxes.

Once the summerhouse was clear Simpson began to scrub and sweep. The following day he painted. A man came the following day to treat the woodwork for damp. The day after that there arrived vans with carpets and furniture. An iron wood burning stove was carefully installed. An electricity cable ran from Dave Marsh's house. Lighting was installed. At the end of the week the summerhouse was transformed into a habitable space. It was money Dave Marsh evidently thought soundly invested.

'I'm not sure if this is what we want,' I said as I looked out at the garden.

'The choice isn't ours,' Caroline replied. 'Dave Marsh doesn't know what he's doing, but he has the right to do it.'

Marsh came over alone that evening. His enthusiasm for the project almost convinced us it was worthwhile. 'I mean, this an example of how the youth of our country can show what's possible. We older people have a lot to learn from the young. No, I feel we often misjudge the young. We shouldn't judge them by those layabouts in the park. Here is an example of something positive, something to be proud of in our young people. Well, more power to their elbow, say I.'

'Sometimes I think in my dreams I've understood. But I wake up to find it's a muddle again. That was, until I met that remarkable young man.'

He impressed us by the thoroughness of his enterprise in making something of the garden. He seemed to know what he was doing. He certainly worked tirelessly in what was promising to be a hot summer. The sweat streaked his soil-darkened face. Yet he took only short breaks only at the hourly intervals he had marked out. He rarely looked across to the house. He seemed oblivious of us, although we suspected that he was hoping to impress us as much as he did.

One day Simpson said, 'If I close my eyes I'm invisible.' Simpson was going to remain a puzzle, but we thought of him as a curiosity within our life, like a plant that has grown by chance, like a bird that has wandered off course, like a creature rarely seen except in the wild.

He seemed restless no longer. So thorough was his work that Simpson seemed to be almost literally developing roots in the garden. He had found a home, a useful task to perform, acceptable neighbours, and a generous patron. He had found a life. Of course it could not last indefinitely. But it was the foundation of something stable, useful and enriching. All the things rebels rejected. All the things Simpson for the time being was developing.

'I can't tell you what a difference that young man has made to my life,' Dave Marsh told us one evening after dinner. 'I've begun to take a more spiritual view of life. I can see that was what was missing in my life. Naturally, I have always had the greatest respect for religion – It doesn't matter which, does it? We all believe in the same God. But I've never been one to delve deep into the mysteries of life. I've got my own philosophy of life, and it's stood me well. But there's more, isn't there? And I want to find it.

'And who am I? Good Neighbour Marsh: councillor and counsellor. Someone reliable. The best sort. Dave Marsh, salt of the earth. A haven in the storm. No-one need know you because you're always there. Good old Dave Marsh. Always read with a drink and laugh.'

We saw him walk across the garden home. We saw him stumble, fall against a tree, and then relieve himself clumsily. Caroline looked away, but I watched Dave Marsh splash himself in the darkness, supposing that he was unseen. He really did think that if he closed his eyes he was invisible.

Four

The ending was not to be as we had imagined. We had anticipated a simple matter of finding somewhere larger, and then finding a buyer for our lease. Farewells to Dave Marsh, with promises to keep in touch, would be the final note of this part of our life together. A last turn in the lock, and a last look at the garden, then Caroline and I would leave for good. It was going to be as simple as that. Such leave takings happen all the time.

But we had forgotten about Simpson and the way he intervened in our life. I had not forgotten about the ear ring. But time had passed without a word said. For all I knew Simpson had forgotten, too. His life, surely, was preoccupied now with Gelina. They had a future together. Trivial incidents of the past and curious ways of gaining temporary advantage must have surrendered to the reality, quite momentous in its way, of his future with Gelina.

Dave Marsh was beginning to regard us as transient creatures now that his new interest was in Simpson and Gelina. They were within his life in a way that Caroline and I were no longer. Once we had been the young couple, fresh and interesting. In so short a time we had faded into a familiarity that allowed Marsh to be fond of us, but in no way intrigued and entertained as he was now by Simpson's articulate mind and Gelina's creative beauty.

'I'll miss the pair of you,' he told us. 'We've had good times.' He was sincere in that, of course. But already he was making his valediction.

The dinner party Marsh held in the autumn was not our farewell. We had some time before going. The party was a welcoming of his new young friends into their new life. The new apartment with its studio was impressive, and we thought them extraordinarily lucky.

I thought Gelina to be quite a talented painter. A series of web-like designs, inspired by an Iris Murdoch novel, were particularly striking. Gelina gave us a copy of *Bruno's Dream*, which neither Caroline nor I had read. Gelina had drawn a web design inside for us. The book was not a loan, but a gift. It was not an expensive gift. That is not the point. The fact of thinking to give it at all was generous, even if there was a motive behind it.

Of course she hoped that Aventurine might exhibit her work. Neither Gelina nor Simpson were going to suggest such a thing. Dave Marsh, of course, had hinted. I told him truthfully that it was possible one day but not yet. 'She has some way to go,' I said. 'But she'll get with persistence.'

'Persistence is everything,' Marsh replied. 'I have every faith in that girl.' That much was evident. It scarcely needed saying. Marsh's predilection for stating the obvious was one of his quite endearing traits that we were going to miss when he was no longer a neighbour.

The wind was shaking the leaves out of the trees.

The air was unseasonably warm, but frosts were predicted within a few days. From the gathering by the river fires could be seen. Shivering in too few clothes, protesters took to begging in the streets. Some busked or juggled as a more dignified way of asking for money.

There was talk of further legal action against the protesters, as there had been during their time in the park. But the hope was that a harsh winter would disperse. Some were going anyway. We saw them on the roads out of town, usually going further west towards Glastonbury and Cornwall, the places where traditionally they might find shelter and fellow-feeling. 'As long they get out of here,' Dave Marsh said. It should be his problem no longer when they were out of the city.

Marsh was concerned that the presence of the Paradise People was affecting business in the city. Aventurine hadn't suffered so far, and I doubted that anywhere had. The city had had its usual high quota of tourists in the summer. Colder weather brought them still, though in lesser numbers of course. Visitors would have noticed a number of young rebels, but for many visitors intent on seeing the sites almost all other people were no more than an ethereal presence. Barred from many places tourists went to, the Paradise People did not register nearly as much as Dave Marsh feared.

That was not the problem for me. It was guiding hand behind the movement that I feared. For I was certain that someone was there, waiting to lead the protesters in a spectacular act of defiance. I wasn't sure quite what that would be. But I was fairly certain something was going to happen.

Caroline didn't agree. She thought the movement no more than a storm that would pass. 'Wait until the winter,' she said. 'Look how Simpson got out,' she continued. 'He knew what he was doing. He's moving on.'

Indeed he was. Where he was going I had no idea. That he had plan was not in doubt. At first I had mistaken him for a dreamer, but knowing him I soon saw how directed he was. So certain about life with all the certainty of youth, and all the energy of a life that knows where it is going. He didn't confide in us, nor Dave Marsh. He didn't confide in anyone, except perhaps Gelina. Simpson seemed to take you into his confidence, but when you looked back he said nothing that revealed his true feelings.

That is not to say he was insincere. He continued to offer his counsel, especially to Marsh who listened in awe and almost in rapture. 'I speak of chance. Why fear what will happen? It's going to happen. It's a question of following our natural impulses. Not every impulse, or it would be chaos. It's a question of trusting to your intuition.'

It interested me much less now. I had heard such things before. Caroline said I wasn't to be too cynical, although she agreed that Simpson was in danger of becoming a bore on the subject of Life.

And yet he was always surprising. That he had seen through the great work of the garden surprised us. That he had found Gelina, that they seem quite settled, that they were intending to develop their ambitions there in the garden, and not to drift as others were drifting – all this amazed us. What we watched was a thread being woven into a pattern.

What we didn't expect is that the pattern would emerge in the way it did, and so quickly. Simpson did not stop from believing there were new worlds to be born. But he was no longer one who had chosen to prophesy in the wilderness. He was making his peace with society even as he hoped it would be transformed by the visionary energies of those who, like himself, saw a different future. There was a song he played, *Inside the Future There'll Be No Time.* We could hear it sometimes when we passed the summerhouse. But that was no longer how he lived his life.

The dinner party was a revelation. Mrs Li had prepared one of her delicious meals, as we had come to expect of her. Mr Li, gravely and deferentially, served at table, carefully pouring the well-chosen wines, including a St Emilion we had brought. Dave Marsh wore a new suit that undoubtedly made the best of him. Rotund, balding and ageing, he none the less did look a more distinguished figure than we had seen of him in a long time.

Caroline, of course, had the charm of her smile, her jewels and her coiffure, all of which brought out the beauty of a mature and elegant woman whom I loved even when I did not understand her. She understood me, and ensured that I was well-presented. She always ensured that.

When Gelina and Simpson entered the room it was

difficult masking our feeling under polite responses. Could these two really be the young bohemians of the summer? The reaction of the Paradise People would have been visceral anger at this betrayal into a polite, ordered world where youth was a matter of fashion rather than rebellion, a world of restraint, decorum and courtesy.

Simpson and Gelina looked the part they clearly wanted to play – pampered and privileged young people, indulging their taste for leisured ease. In his velvet suit Simpson complemented Gelina in her silk gown, hair pompadoured, poised as carefully she seated herself, the hint of a spoiled pout as artfully seductive as the generous spread of her hips.

'Well,' said Marsh, 'this is an honour.' I added a murmur of appreciation. It was Caroline who was more bold and generous in her praise. 'Absolutely enchanting,' she said. 'And, Simpson, you look so smart. Don't they both look wonderful, darling?' she said, turning to me, expecting me to agree with fulsome praise matching her own.

There was a story Simpson told about walking down the street and hearing woman singing a forgotten song, *Sì, Sì, Señor*. It was trite and stale, but the woman sang the song with such feeling that it made Simpson stop walking, forget what he was doing, and listen to her. It was only for a moment. Then it was gone.

I thought back to the way seven or eight years before, of the time when we began to settle down, willing to compromise, eager to be accepted as Simpson and

Gelina were willing and eager now. What once would have been dismissed soon became the way we naturally were. Like falling in love, it happened all the time.

An essential part of it was to do with love. Youth is sure to question. Questioning, youth is sure to become angry. Then love intervenes, if we are lucky, and something creative appears when the anger is transmuted into passion. Simpson and Gelina were adorned with desire made acceptable by its decorum. But the erotic charge was there undeniably. I thought of Caroline and I dressing for the evening, exchanging admiring glances. Caroline had tamed my passions, and channelled my desires in ways that bound me to her.

Love had given me a sense of freedom, and yet I could feel bonds that I willingly accepted. Of course, there had been the evening with Ruth, the secret moment when I strayed so slightly, the night in the summerhouse when I thought I was unseen. I didn't want to remember that. It was nothing. But it was everything if Caroline were to learn of it. The trust would be loosened. The love would fade. We would drift apart as surely as now we were coming together again.

That Gelina in her elegance stirred the blood Caroline was well aware. But she could deal with that in her artful way. It was Dave Marsh we pitied. His blood stirred without hope of satisfactory release. He was older, of course, and less given to the urgency that struck a younger man. But tonight he was going to retire to a lonely bed with only scotch for comfort.

Or perhaps he wouldn't even reach the bed before

collapsing, as he had been known to do in his drawing room, if not yet in public. Then it was Mr Li's task to put his master to bed without a word said in the morning.

Dave Marsh had known love, and had lost it. His story was a cautionary tale of the folly of the self-satisfied. For Gelina's benefits he told the story again over dinner. 'I got the shock of my life,' he began, 'when I saw what the noise from the swimming pool was all about. She was deliberately humiliating me in the worst possible way. I've never seen such a display.' He took another gulp of the St Emilion. 'Good wine this. Anyway, as I say, that was how it ended. I could have understood the whole thing more had he been white.'

'How awful for you, Mr Marsh.'

'Call me Dave, my dear. Well, awful isn't the word. I thought I'd go mad with the shame. I'd certainly never go back there again on holiday. I had a word with the manager. He seemed to understand. Well, imagine my position. Of course I was prepared to forgive her, but it was never the same after that.'

'How terrible for you, Dave.'

'I said if a word of this gets out my career in business and politics will be in ruins. She just laughed. Laughed. In my face. After that she laughed at everything I said. Until finally she didn't even laugh. She just sat there. It was the silence I couldn't bear. And the way her eyes seemed to be judging me. And beats me to this day what I'd done wrong. I mean, she had everything she could possibly want. What more could she possibly want except to bloody well wreck my life, and all because of one night – one night, mark you – that I deeply regret to this day. A better woman would have understood, but not madam. Oh no, not madam.'

I thought that Simpson shot me a glance. My recollection is that, fleetingly, perhaps involuntarily, he did look in my direction. I certainly did not look in his direction, for I did not dare. Caroline would have noticed something happening. I was alarmed at the thought that she might suspect something. One suspicion leads to another. I remembered the ear ring found in the summerhouse.

'Dave,' Simpson responded to break the uneasy silence, 'you must never blame yourself. Had she truly loved you she would have forgiven you. Things happen in the night. Mistakes are made. You must forgive yourself.'

'Well, I can't forgive her, not after that public humiliation.'

'Of course,' Simpson replied, 'the two situations can't be compared. A little drunken fumbling in the dark is entirely different from the display in the swimming pool.'

'Exactly so, young man. You're wise beyond your years. You've got a good man there, Gelina.' Marsh replenished everyone's drinks. When it came to Gelina he hesitated. His whole frame quivered for a moment. Desire, rigorously suppressed, had shown itself.

'It's getting rather chilly in here,' Caroline said, covering for Marsh.

'Well, perhaps if we find ourselves somewhere comfortable in the drawing room. I believe there's a good fire in there – and more wine, of course. This is an evening to remember.'

Marsh was stumbling as he walked. This was an evening likely to end in his collapse.

'Where,' he asked, 'would I be without my friends? Good friends I know I can rely on?'

Earlier he had spoken fulsomely in praise of Gelina's art. His praise would have been as fulsome had her work been awkward or false. Dave Marsh had no knowledge of art. The pictures on his walls were chosen for him. Indeed, it was his custom that enabled Aventurine to prosper when it first opened. That was how he and I met. He was buying art not only for himself but for the country club he was thinking of investing in. We sold him more than we dared hope would be possible. That was how Aventurine survived its first year. After that, on Dave Marsh's recommendation, others came forward, and our survival was guaranteed. I owed Dave Marsh my prosperity.

We owed Dave Marsh much. Caroline and I could have survived on her salary from the library, but we could never have afforded the life we enjoyed. Our debt to him accounted for our tolerance of him even as he spoke as he did. All his behaviour was bad when you think about it. But he had a generous heart. It was a generous heart in a selfish mind. He didn't understand the world.

This gave him an innocence in contrast to Simpson's knowingness that never allowed me to trust him entirely. To that lack of trust was added my fear, for he had never surrendered the ear ring. I feared his motives. I wanted Simpson to disappear.

Geoffrey Heptonstall

Five

And so he did. Simpson was the man who went to the limits of the known world, the man who sailed across the vast water, the man last seen climbing the great mountain, the man who attempted crossing the forbidden waste. There were convicts in Australia who perished in an impossible bid to reach China. Escape into the bush, and certain death, was preferable to a life in the penal colony. There were men – it was invariably men – who died in attempts to fly, usually from church towers. Columbus records how his crew was on the verge of mutiny when evidence of approaching land appeared in the water. All such pioneers hope to be Columbus. They die at the death of such hopes.

It was a kind of death he suffered. He had said that the old self has to die for the new self to live. That was one of the least original of his wisdoms, although there was some truth in it. But it was too obvious a thought. More original was his coda: 'We must die three times.' That I did find interesting. It resonated with me in a way that little of Simpson's esoteric wisdom did. The power of the magic number three had worked on me in spite of my doubts. I never forgot what Simpson said.

When first I encountered Simpson in the garden his thoughts made me think. For that I was grateful. At the end of his time in the garden he was making me think again. For that, too, I was grateful. For other things a lurking resentment had soured my feelings about him.

I was angry with him because of the ear ring. But it was more than that which irritated me. I envied his ability to make things happen. What had happened in my life had been by effort with the occasional fortunate chance. With Simpson it was all luck. How could I not be envious and resentful?

Of course envy is a weakness. When I was a boy of eleven or twelve a cousin of mine was going to be taken to New York. I became envious. I felt at one moment when family talk was once more of this trip a pang of intense jealousy. Covering my feelings with a joke, I reflected, even at so young an age, on how poisonous that intense pang was. I knew it was wrong. It was better, I thought, not to resent others. It was better to wait until my turn came. My turn did come after some years. It was worth the wait, a wait not soured by resentment, but leavened by expectations. If my turn had never come at least my life would not have been diminished by the devil of envy.

Yet with Simpson it was not so easy to let the feeling go. Sometimes the devil must be given his due. I couldn't deny that a part of me envied Simpson his youth, his ease, his charm, his luck. At thirty, I felt the onset of age. For how much longer could we think of ourselves as young? We were young, but already there was another generation rising behind us.

It must be a familiar story to many. There comes that time when we realize that the torch is passing from our hands. It happens when a new rock star appears on the scene. The stars we knew from the past have not gone, but there is this interloper whom people only a few years younger than we are like more than we do. We dismiss this as a phenomenon that is sure to pass. It isn't, as we well know. Did we really think that time had stopped? Did we really think that we would have the last word?

There came in stark reality that trespasser in the garden who smiled as he took charge of the situation. That smile told us it was time to accept what we already knew. Caroline and I were going to go. We were going to disappear, leaving Simpson to enjoy the comforts of his situation.

It had to happen. Perhaps I willed it to happen. Thinking back it could have been another way.

'Come up when you're ready,' Caroline had said, making her way upstairs. I ought to have followed her. Then my life should have been different. That is to say it should have been the same. We can't predict anything for certain. There are likelihoods. It was likely that Caroline and I would go on living for a while in this place.

But I remained curious about the noise in the garden, for I was certain it was an intruder rather than a harmless creature of the night. I went down to the garden, and entered a different world.

Had I not gone down Simpson might have left the garden, making his way through the night to wherever he could find refuge. Resourceful, he was sure to have found a niche somewhere. We simply made things easier for him. We created his luck. It was our fault. It was my fault.

What was it Simpson had said? 'I wanted to escape. It was getting tired of doing nothing. I hate doing nothing.' He wanted to do everything. 'If I have a choice I'd like time to think,' he said. 'I have no difficulty in accepting that here is where I'm to be for a while. I've no difficulty with something which brings people together, especially in a natural environment. Communication is very important. Life at the moment is about creating a network of ideas and resources so that when the time is right we can change. We can change everything.'

These were thoughts passing through the nebulae which drifted across the city as if from Lyonesse. Soon such thoughts should pass us by. Anchored in our determined life, Caroline and I could leave Marsh to believe whatever consolations he might choose. Simpson would tire of him before he tired of Simpson. Of that we had no doubt.

The Centre for Enlightenment that Simpson hoped to found would be at least as expensive as Gelina's studio. It was Marsh's free wish to spend his money in these ways. 'You see,' Marsh explained, 'money is about helping people. It's about enabling lives to be lived in better. Simpson can put it better than me. But you know what I mean. I understand now the spiritual value of money.'

It was as if Marsh also was drifting through the sky. 'At times I feel I can touch the moon. Do you ever feel that? I do now. I never did before.'

'Exactly so, Dave,' Simpson agreed. 'Have faith in

yourself. Trust yourself, and you'll be able to trust others. But you know that already I'm sure. You're not beginning your journey. It began a long time ago.'

It seemed that Simpson possessed an infinite capacity for these aphorisms. He had an answer for every question. Often he would both ask the question and supply the answer. It was clever without being profound. It got on my nerves so much now that I found it unbearable. I longed for Simpson to disappear.

When it happened I had what I wished, but not in the way I had hoped. Of course it was not the way I wished it to be. It never is, is it? The reality was far worse than any imagining. I had envisaged Dave Marsh hurrying across the lawn, his face drained of colour, his hands trembling as he spoke of the shocking news. He would say, 'Simpson's gone. The bugger's just gone without a word said. I can't believe it.'

My commiseration would be a mere formality. No serious harm had been done. Marsh was going to recover from the shock. It wasn't a bereavement. And there would be peace again in this place in the remaining time we had.

It might have been that Marsh suggested we move into the cottage he had built for Gelina and Simpson. It might have been that we should have accepted. Of that I can't be sure. The point is that the thread would be broken. Life should return to its familiar pattern of domestic tranquillity whatever was happening down there among all the discontent.

As if life were the way we planned it. In reality the

thread was more tortuous than the simple narrative of my imaginings.

The next time we saw Marsh his face flushed either with excitement or embarrassment or, more likely, both combined. He had invited us to Gelina's studio now that it was complete.

Simpson, we noticed, was not there. We supposed he would be coming later after some unexpected delay. But, no, there was to be no Simpson in the studio, not on this nor on any subsequent occasion. The reason was evident enough in the way to our amazement Marsh slipped his arm round Gelina's waist. The way she accepted his squeeze – the poise of her body leaning towards him – was everything Marsh had dreamed for without ever expecting it was going to happen. Twice her age, and no match for her in looks, intellect or talent, Marsh had won his prize simply by offering her everything she wanted.

In a corner alone he explained his feelings to me. 'I know what you're thinking. But I had to follow my heart. It's what that young man always said. He's fully accepted it. It's what I want. It's what Evangelina wants. Now, how many young men would give their wholehearted blessing in the way he did? He'll go far, you know. He's one in ten million, believe me.'

There was nothing I could think to say. Not a word would come. Rarely do we find ourselves genuinely speechless. But at that moment I was speechless.

'I suppose it's all to do with the way life is. If we follow our heart, well, it leads us where it will. I'm not one to talk about destiny because I believe we make our own decisions. After all, my philosophy is one of freedom – responsible freedom, mind. But... I think you know what I'm trying to get at.'

I didn't care what Marsh was getting at. As much as I had hoped Simpson might go, I could not condone the way it had happened. The sight of Marsh and Gelina was wrong, hopelessly wrong. I felt, against my will, a touch of sympathy for Simpson, for I didn't believe that he had given his blessing wholeheartedly. There would be a deep hurt inside. That was only natural.

My sincere hope was that Simpson would emerge as a better man out of this hurt. Perhaps, I reflected, such a crisis was exactly what he needed to burst that confidence so that a fuller, deeper human being emerged from the ashes of his aphorisms. But that did not lessen the grievous harm done to him.

I feared for what Simpson might do. All measure of possibilities paraded through my mind. In the end, however, Simpson did nothing. Or, rather, he did none of the things one might have anticipated. He vanished.

Or so I thought. Then came the night in the garden when I heard a noise as I had heard a noise those few, long months before. It was Simpson, of course. Who else could it have been? He must have waited night after night until I appeared alone. It was late in the year. Those vigils in the dark must have been miserable. Only a very determined man could have waited as he did.

That was when I saw the true Simpson emerged

from the chrysalis of his ethereal charm. There was a harder man coming out. The shock of betrayal had matured him for better or worse. The work of a few years was accomplished in a few weeks. The thought of this chilled me more than the December air on my face.

'This is a surprise,' he said.

'Not really,' I replied. 'I'm not surprised you're back. But you're not going to do anything, are you?'

'You mean, like hurt Dave Marsh? Or Gelina? No, I want nothing more to do with them. It's you I want to see.'

'I had no part in...'

'I know that. But there's the little matter of the ear ring.' From his pocket Simpson produced the ear ring. There was sufficient light for me to see it sparkle. 'You see, you betrayed Caroline. And I know what it's like to be betrayed.'

'It was only...'

'It was only a betrayal.'

'A little fumbling in the dark was the phrase you used, Simpson.'

'You think you can get away with it. Caroline will never know. The two of you can go through life with the secret of all your betrayals – because there'll be others – all your betrayals safely hidden. I can't allow that.'

Simpson's face was hidden by shadows. I couldn't look into his eyes as I should have wished. He was a silhouette with a cold, determined voice pronouncing judgements he had no right to make. He sounded authoritative about matters for which he had no mature experience. That made him dangerous.

'But it doesn't matter to you,' I protested.

'Everything matters to me. Everything. Especially the things that I have to see, to live with. They matter to me.'

'Do you think you are a divine emissary who can judge the rest of us? Do you think you are perfect?'

There was an intake of breath, perhaps a sigh, a measured exasperation before he spoke again. 'Everything matters to me because everything that happens affects me as surely as it affects you.'

'Everything?'

'Everything.'

'There's no area of doubt? No, of course not.'

'If I close my eyes I'm invisible,' came the mocking reply as Simpson retreated into the bushes. From there I saw his arm lifted. He appeared to be throwing something towards the house. I supposed it to be the ear ring. 'Will that save your marriage?' he asked. 'I doubt it.'

'Just go. You've no place here. You no longer matter. You can't control our lives. Just go.' I trusted that my voice didn't betray my fear. My fear of Simpson lingered even as the ear ring fell into the night. The chances of it being found in our remaining time were remote. And even if it were found some explanation could be given. That was no longer a concern. But fear of Simpson had entered my bloodstream. I could not feel at ease in his presence, certainly not now that he was vengeful and mad. The anger would pass through him in time. Until then he was a danger, especially to himself.

He had disappeared into dark. I heard another voice. A man's voice. Some else was there, but I didn't know who. And then there was a noise, a kind of whispered scream. Hurrying toward the sound, I could see nothing. There was no-one there. Simpson had indeed disappeared. He had fallen off the edge of our world, down into Paradise Park. Whether he had slipped or jumped I couldn't know. What mattered was that he was gone. This time he was gone.

Two:

Ghosts

50

One

'I've just had my ex-wife's second husband's ex-wife on the phone asking me who I think has custody of the children. I said which children of which marriage? And I wasn't trying to be funny. Considering her sense of humour that is just as well. So she's calls me a complete tosser. I say I'm simply seeking clarification. Then she tells me not to be so fuckin' stupid, and slams down the phone. So I'm no wiser as to what's going on.'

Dave Marsh was sitting in his office one morning in the spring. There was a time when the conversation would have irritated him intensely. Today he merely laughed. Marsh was able to laugh at many things. The world had changed. His life had changed. His business had prospered. He had found love. For the better part of two years life had been kinder to him for longer than he had known before in a life that had known so much disadvantage and so many reversals. In the past at the moment he thought all was well something went wrong. But now that was no longer the case. Everything went right and had kept going right. He was a contented man untroubled by minor irritations.

'It'll sort itself out, I dare say.' He dared say this because things had a habit of sorting themselves out. Marsh had no worries now. The world had changed for the better. It was almost better than he could believe possible.

Of course Marsh remained a man of opinions. He

would have called himself a man of conviction. Not everything had changed. It was not yet a perfect world. 'Women, they don't know what they want. Evangelina's different, of course. She's one in a million. The rest of them don't know what they want, but, by Heaven, they're going to get it. And they're going to get it at any price. Women, they've no conscience, you know, no bloody conscience. Wife and present company excepted.' Marsh glanced at Jackie, his tolerant and loyal personal assistant.

Jackie took the visitor's coat. He was standing in the doorway, having arrived punctually at eleven. 'But I'm forgetting my manners,' Marsh said, shaking the visitor's hand, and offering him a chair. 'Some coffee, Jackie, I think. And we'll not want to be disturbed.'

I sat down the other side of Marsh's desk. 'It's good to see you again. How are things? How's Caroline?'

'The last time I heard from her she was well,' I said. 'She went back home. I don't see her.' The truth was that I didn't hear from her.

'I didn't realize.'

'It's been a while. Not long after we moved,' I explained. 'It simply wasn't the same. We were happy in your place. It fell apart after we moved.'

'I'm very sorry to hear that. I thought you two were rock solid. Sure of it.'

'Things change.'

'Ah yes, not everyone's as fortunate as me, that's true,' Marsh said. 'But I suppose life is what you make it.'

'You've done well, Dave.'

'I've done very well, young man.' Marsh scrutinized my face as he spoke. Very likely he was trying to work out my age now. He was thinking how I had aged a little. He was thinking that, despite my loss of Caroline, I looked well. He was forgetting that Caroline had gone some time before. And he had no idea of the life I had now.

To Marsh I was the man he'd known in a context that was long past. The house may have crumbled, and the garden turned to wilderness (though I doubted these things). I had never been back. I had lost touch with Marsh. I had lost touch with the life I had, as I knew I would. In Marsh's mind I was like a man in a photograph forever fixed in one position, never moving, never changing, never growing older, and never looking younger.

Then it came to me as I sat in his office, that I was no longer alive in his eyes. He didn't know me. I was the past. He was going back three or four years. The time in between had been for him so fulfilling that the past was a distant, dark age, a time to remember or to forget. It was a time that no longer touched him.

I doubted if Marsh cared what I was doing or where I was living and how I was living. He was the wrong person for me to see at this time. He was the wrong person to see at any time.

But it was Marsh who had summoned me. To my surprise I got a call from Aventurine's main gallery in Walcot Street. Someone called Councillor Marsh (an important man) was looking for me. He had a business proposition, an important one that was going to be very advantageous for the gallery. But he wished to speak to me, and only to me. I was an old friend, he had said. He needed someone he knew to be reliable. 'No offence, young lady, of course.' I pictured Marsh flustered by his ineptitude, desperate to get things right.

'They told me you weren't living here now. For a moment I was afraid you'd moved out of the business.'

'No,' I explained, 'we opened another gallery in Wells. I'm there.'

'They told me. Doing well, the new gallery?'

'Very well,' I told him truthfully. 'It was a gamble that paid off.'

'You've got to take risks in business. It's the same thing in politics, really. Same thing in life. As long you're careful you don't fall ov...'

Jackie came in with the coffee at a coincidentally appropriate moment. There were things in the past neither Marsh nor I wanted to mention.

'I suppose there's money down there in Wells. There's money here, of course. Property prices now! Not that I'm complaining, of course. High prices mean prosperity, and who can complain at that?'

Marsh had gained weight since we last met. He had lost some hair, and what remained was white. This gave him the look of a man of indeterminate age, in reasonable health, and apparently a contented life. Gone, I supposed, were the rages against the woman who had betrayed him. Gone, I supposed, was the bitterness that had soured his view of the world. In place of that was a benevolence, or so it seemed, that accounted for his wish to contact me after such a long time.

I guessed that business was the primary motive. He seemed genuinely pleased to see me, and no doubt he was pleased, but there was sure to be a commercial motive. Dave Marsh understood two things: money and power, in so far as he made a clear distinction between the two. I felt certain that there was to be some proposition in mind. All else was the sociable preliminary.

Neither of us wanted to speak about Simpson. There was an unspoken understanding between us. If there was one name guaranteed to cloud Dave Marsh's day, and to destroy any prospect of business between us, it would be mention of Simpson. Both Marsh and I had reasons for not talking about him.

There was an air of guilt still in the recesses of my mind about Simpson. How much more so would that be true of Marsh? I had failed to save Simpson from his fall, although in my defence it was dark when he fell. I could have warned him, perhaps. Could I have warned him? I could have said something. But he moved so quickly in the dark. He sped into the bushes, laughing maniacally. He was giddy with hurt pride and vengeance. It was likely to end in some disaster. I ought to have known.

Caroline never forgave me. She was not a witness. There was no witness. But she was vexed by my failure. She blamed me for what happened. That was unfair. The possibility was that even had I warned him to be careful at the cliff's edge Simpson would not have heard, or if he had heard me it is probable he wouldn't have heeded me. He willed his fall, I thought. He wanted it to happen. I knew him well enough to recognize that much about him.

But Caroline felt differently. Of course Simpson's fall may have been no more than an excuse. Blaming me was a way for Caroline to justify her sense of detachment from me. The move to a new place was to be a new beginning. But there could be no beginning. The time had come for change.

As for Marsh, there was the guilt, I supposed, about Gelina. This always had seemed to me far worse than anything I had done or failed to do. What was my guilt compared with Marsh's? That is, of course, if Marsh let himself explore his conscience. This I doubted. Knowing Marsh, and seeing him now, he did not seem a troubled man. If Gelina had tried to ease his conscience, her charm had worked. It was, after all, Gelina's free choice to leave a penniless young man without prospects for an older, richer man with contacts. It was her choice.

I suspected that it was she who made the first move. How could Marsh have resisted some late-night suggestion of secret pleasures? Gelina, inviting with a blend of submissive odalisque and commanding chatelaine, would have found Marsh such easy prey. How could he have resisted?

It was very likely his memory of that first night was clouded even at the time. Now, of course, he would say that Gelina had been ready to move on. Simpson had none of the experience to satisfy the many demands and desires of a girl like Gelina. And in that Marsh would say no more than the truth, even if the truth encompassed the betrayal of a friend whose help and counsel Marsh had once welcomed.

'But it's not just about money, you know,' Marsh continued. 'One thing I've learned is the value of money. Prosperity buys freedom. It buys choice, and all the chances that enhance life. Poverty's like prison. Prosperity is the means to a better life. There's no other way of seeing it.'

'Quite.'

'You're not convinced, are you? I'm surprised. An intelligent man like you, an educated white man, should be able to see what I'm saying is correct. Of course you do. You'd not be here if you didn't know that what I say is right. I might not have all the education, but I know about priorities, believe me. I just wish this new government did. Too left wing for my liking, and for most people's liking. And there we were thinking Socialism's a thing of the past, a nightmare we can put behind us. People'll not put up with it, you know. It goes the natural instincts of the English character.'

We both sipped our coffee in silence. On a social level I had nothing now to say to Marsh. Indifferent to his life now, I probably let my boredom show, although I tried to feign an interest. I didn't try as hard as I would have done had I cared about the possibility of doing busy with Dave Marsh.

'Wealth isn't just money,' I said.

'Agreed.'

'Wealth is also about values, about culture, about faith.'

'Definitely. Definitely. No doubt about it. I mean you look at the wealth that is our national heritage. That cathedral of yours in Wells. This beautiful city. But we need money to live. You can't live without money, now, can you? You must admit that.'

This was reminiscent of the conversations we had in the past. They were conversations that went nowhere. I knew it would conclude with Marsh defending 'all that is good about my country.'

'Let's move on, Dave. This isn't the time.' I hoped sincerely that I didn't sound too abrupt. Evidently I didn't.

'Y-yes, of course. Sorry, I do get carried away,' Marsh, surprisingly, agreed. And in agreeing with that note of hesitation and its subsequent apologetic note I saw the first sign of vulnerability in the new Dave Marsh. It surprised me.

The possibility occurred to me then that Marsh's true motive in summoning me was to demonstrate how successful he was. Gone was the unfulfilled ambition In its place came the benign, well-loved public figure. At least, that was the image he wanted to convey. If that really were Marsh's motive it was a foolish one, certain to end in disaster. I knew him well enough to sense the desperation.

For a long time there was nothing said, and I wondered if there was anything to say. To break the silence

I said, 'You have some proposal, Dave?'

'That first wife of mine,' Marsh replied after another long pause, 'she was always undermining the little schemes I had. Pipe-dreams she called them. Well, one or two might have been, but the point is that I had ideas. I had a wealth of ideas, you might say.'

This was not going well. I wanted Marsh to come to the point, if there was a point. He had shown that there was the old fool behind the new fool. I ought not to have been surprised.

'I've a new venture. It's something that might interest you professionally if not personally, possibly both. We'll see. Anyway, I have a new scheme in mind. More than in mind, actually. I've signed the lease on the property. It's a lovely old house. You might know it. I've pictures of it here. It's in Combe Melbury. That's near you, isn't it? Melbury Hall. Has a nice ring to it, I think. The attraction for me is its seclusion. For this venture of mine I need somewhere secluded. Another country club, but this is to be a country club with a difference.' Marsh paused, this time for effect. As I looked up from the photographs Marsh's eyes met mine. He was saying something with his eyes. 'As I say, it needs seclusion. Somewhere well away from busybodies. You know how word gets out, and people get the wrong idea.'

Marsh looked beyond me to the door. He wanted to be sure it was firmly closed. I didn't like the direction this conversation was going. Knowing Marsh as I did, I suspected his scheme was not one I could feel at ease with.

'You see men with responsibilities need somewhere where they can get away, somewhere well away from their cares and stresses. You know what it's like with business worries, family worries. There's this and there's that. It all mounts up. A man needs somewhere he can go to relax, to feel at ease, to feel valued. He needs to feel human again. And the best way he can do that is by being a man. It's only natural for a man to be a man. You know what I mean?'

'I think so.'

'Of course you bloody do.' Marsh coughed to cover his lapse of judgement. This was, as he would have put it, a delicate matter. He dared not be clumsy. 'I mean, you're a man, a young man. You understand what I'm getting at, old friend?'

'Well, of course.'

'But, as I say, people can get the wrong idea. You know how people like to gossip, to speculate and ex-aggerate. There are plenty of people with dirty minds. And, believe me, in business as well as politics, you make enemies. If you make a go of things there's many an envious bastard who'd do you down. So that's why I need people I can rely on. People like yourself. People I know and trust.'

'So how can I help?'

'I thought you'd never ask. It's a question of art. Melbury Hall is going to need some art. There'll be tasteful décor and furnishings, of course. But, person-ally, I like a bit of art on the walls. Art of all kinds, as long as it's art and not something to give a sane man nightmares.'

'When you say art, Dave...?'

'I mean art. Have no fear about that. There'll be plenty of entertainment at Melbury Hall, have no fear.' Marsh's face coloured as he laughed. Some embarrassment troubled him before he recovered his composure with a glass of iced water.

Jackie knew how to provide these things without being asked. That was her secret; she made herself indispensable. She was so discreet. Later I got to know her quite well when she became friendly with Rissa. I respected Jackie. I came to value what she said - and what she didn't say.

'But I want the place to have some class,' Marsh continued, having cooled down. 'You see, I want our members to feel they're in safe hands. Tasteful décor, as I say. There'll be some pretty high-class people, I'm determined on that. Oh, and there'd be free membership for you, need I add, should you ever wish to grace us with your presence. As I say, there'll be plenty of entertainment to suit all. Have no fear of that.'

I had doubt of that, nor of the nature of the entertainment. As for the art we could provide, I had doubts about that. 'Surely Gelina...?' I began.

'Ah, no. Not Evangelina. For one thing, I don't think it would be quite right to involve her somehow. I just wouldn't feel comfortable about that,' Marsh replied predictably. 'And, in any case, she's in California at this moment in time. I'm flying out there myself on Saturday. It's been a very successful exhibition. Well, I have you in part to thank for the success of her career. And don't you be modest. You invested time on her when I doubt if anyone else would have. As you know, it paid off handsomely.'

'I'm sure you'd have found another gallery. Gelina's a great talent.'

'Well, I'd like to think so. She's doing well over there. First New York, now California. They say Santa Monica's wonderful. Well, I'll be finding out in a day or two.' Anticipating my response to his proposal, Marsh added, 'You can give me your answer when I get back from California. You'll need time to mull it over, I dare say.'

'I can give you my answer now, Dave,' I said, slowly rising from the chair.

The look Dave Marsh gave me was as cold as any look I have ever seen. The benign countenance surrendered to a resentment that was almost reassuringly familiar from the past.

'But what is there to discuss?' he said. He had not anticipated anything but immediate acceptance. He had been so sure in his mind that I was going to accept a very lucrative commission. How could I hesitate for a second? All I needed to think about were the practical arrangements. What else was there to discuss? It was obvious that I was going to accept with the gratitude this favour from an old friend who was prepared to put so much business my way. It was an honour for me to think that a successful and important man like Dave Marsh trusted me above everything he could have approached. How could I possibly think of betraying him, after all we had meant to one another in the past? How could I be so mean and stupid?

'I'd need to consider this,' I said by way of conciliation.

'Rubbish. It's a good offer, and you'll not get better. I'm prepared to pay a good price. There's many a gallery, I'm sure, that'd leap for what I'm giving you on a plate, and you turn to me bold as bloody brass and tell me you need to consider it. I thought you had more sense. Well, I know one thing, that wife of your would've told you to take it.'

'Aventurine's a partnership,' I began to explain. 'We never take major decisions without some discussion.'

'Yes, I understand that. I'm in business myself, you know. But, let's face it, that's just a formality. No, I don't expect a definite answer until you've discussed it with the girls. But that's not what you're saying, is it?'

'I'm not sure about it, Dave.'

'Well,' he said in conclusion, 'you needn't think I'm a pushover.'

There was no handshake before I left, nor was there the least hope that we would ever speak again on this on any other matter. It had been a mistake to revisit the past, a mistake we both had made. Surely we must have guessed that it was going to end in anger or recriminations? There was so much history neither of us wanted to remember, but which neither of us could forget. That, perhaps, is the nature of history, especially when it between old friends whose friendship has faded with time.

Geoffrey Heptonstall

Two

After that I didn't want to think much more of Dave Marsh. I certainly wanted nothing more to do with him. It had been a mistake to see him. I surely knew it would be a mistake.

'Of course you knew it would be a mistake,' Rissa said. My memories of Marsh now were soured. I thought him not merely a fool (always he had been that) but dangerous. There was a hint of something sinister in the way he spoke of the Melbury project. It was morally dubious, of course. There was something in the way. Marsh spoken about it that made me very uneasy. In the days and weeks to come as I thought of it, and I talked of it with Rissa.

She had never met Dave Marsh. She had heard vaguely of Councillor Marsh from local gossip. I had spoken of him from time to time, although that part of my life was not so important now that I was elsewhere with someone else. The book of Caroline was closing as Rissa came closer to me, and I to her.

Rissa had the advantage of never having known, and never having seen, the things I spoke of. She could look objectively. She accepted I had no part in Simpson's fall. 'It was dark, and he was crazy. He was going to do something mad,' she said. She was right.

As for Marsh, she agreed that there was a strange undertone to the sound of the Melbury project. 'I mean, with someone like that business and politics and pleasure are all combined, aren't they? He wants something, and it's not just money, and it's not just women. He wants something he doesn't have yet.'

'What?' I asked. 'Perhaps he doesn't know.'

'He knows,' Rissa said. 'It's power. He wants to be a powerful figure.'

'You mean something more than the city council.'

'I mean a lot more. Maybe he's not worked out all the details. He's lazy and not too bright so he won't know what he wants exactly. But he's got an idea. And that's what Melbury's all about.'

'You mean inviting powerful types?'

'Yeah. Melbury's the honey jar. See if I'm right.'

'We'll never know.'

'We'll know all about it when the power goes to his head.'

'You could be right.'

'I am right.'

Rissa took pride in being right. Her perceptions were sharper than mine, less illusioned. She was younger than I, but more experienced in the how the world works. She understood how things were. Had Rissa known him, I doubt if she would have had any time for Dave Marsh. I was sure she would have had no time for Simpson.

'You go on about this Simpson,' she said. 'But he's a two a penny New Age guru. The world's full of them.'

'He had a way with him,' I said, defending myself rather than Simpson.

'Well, his sort always do,' Rissa replied. 'He takes

you into his confidence.'

'It was Dave Marsh he convinced.'

'Sure. Marsh was intellectually the weaker, and emotionally more vulnerable. Marsh was easy prey.'

How could I have disagreed when Rissa spoke the obvious truth? She spoke it so clearly. There was no forgiving caution in her voice when she mentioned Simpson. She had taken an instant dislike to him. Her view never wavered: 'He was clever in a superficial way. Arrogant, too. And he was playing games. He deserved to lose. It served him right. I mean, it's not as if he died.'

'He was lucky. I suspect most of the damage was to his ego. His family took him away once he was out of hospital. I heard he was in Los Angeles. His family has money.'

'But of course.'

'Now I don't know what he's up to or where he is,' I added.

'Do you care?'

'It was a while ago. He'll have changed.'

'Are you sure about that? He may look quite different. He'll be older. He may act differently. But he won't have changed inside – except, of course, for the worse.'

'Rissa, you always speak as if you knew him.'

'Well, I know the type. Anyway, I think I did see him. From your description I think I did see him.'

Rissa told me the story of her time when she first graduated, was back home in the West Country, working in a restaurant, and looking for some direction in her life. One night very late after the restaurant had closed she had gone with friends to the riverside where the Paradise People were encamped. Her friends and she had gone out of amused curiosity to see for themselves what these people were like behind the publicity they had attracted.

In blue-jeans and jerseys Rissa and her friends mingled with the Paradise People, many of whom were awake, sitting by their fires. They drank and smoked quietly. There was the inevitable sound of someone in the distance strumming a guitar. A girl was singing to herself. One man was stumbling about, cursing the world. He soon passed on his way to his tent. Most tents were dark, but others had lanterns or candles outside, indicating that visitors were welcome. Rissa and her friends chose not to visit any of them.

'Ladies,' a man said, 'come keep me company, all of you.' It was then that Rissa grew concerned that this outing had not been such a good idea. She said nothing to the others for the moment, but kept a watchful eye out for trouble.

'I know you, don't I?' someone asked. He had an authoritative tone. His answer demanded a reply. When he was satisfied that the visitors were neither reporters nor officials he suggested they sit by the fire. 'You'll be safe,' he assured them. 'While ever I'm here you'll be safe. This is a peace camp. It's about freedom. You understand what I'm saying?' And he did seem reassuring.

The conversation was desultory, and Rissa was soon bored. One man bedded down for the night in his sleeping bag by the fire. He told his friend of a bad experience in London where strangers turned out to be predators. 'You get funny types there in London. You're safe here,' the man's friend said, just as the other man had assured Rissa and her friends.

What struck Rissa's attention was a young man she saw moving about the camp, speaking to everyone purposefully. Finally he came to the fire. He spoke to John, the reassuring figure. Their conversation was at some distance, and could not be overheard. Several times the young man looked towards the fire where the girls sat until John came over, saying, 'Actually, I think it's time for you to leave. You're welcome another time, but we all need to crash now.' That was clearly untrue, but, politely, John wanted them to go away.

Rissa was secretly pleased. The atmosphere had been, she said, strange. There was an air of something about to happen. The young man who wanted them to go was not safe and reassuring. Could that really have been Simpson? It was very perplexing if it were he. Yet at the same time it made more sense of things. Simpson as a man without loyalties was a more dangerous man than the genial figure in the garden. The true Simpson was emerging.

As for the Paradise People, 'They'll wander for ever,' Rissa said of them. It was the sort of thing Caroline would have said, although the two women had little in common. Rarely was I reminded of Caroline in the things Rissa said and did, or in the way she looked and talked. They were completely separate and different people whom I never confused. But when it came to the Paradise People Rissa was as sharp in her disdain as Caroline. 'They'll wander for ever unless they find a leader.'

They did wander. They were to be seen on all the roads, especially the ones that led to ancient places, or sacred sites. We saw them pass through, mendicant pilgrims in search of solace perhaps, or simply food and shelter. Somewhere out there to the west was a place where they could find all the things they needed in life. These things would be given freely, as was to be the way of living in the age to come. They were travellers to a dawn of peace and plenty. Soon it would happen. Then there would be no more wandering and searching. They would come soon upon a land that was theirs, a land where they belonged. When they reached that land they would know it at once. They would be welcomed, garlanded and honoured. All who entered would be treated as brothers and sisters of the sacred family of God's children.

There was one more hill to climb, one more river to cross, one more forest to pass through. There was one more night to spend on the road toward the dawn. Then they would wake to see the celestial vision shimmering on the horizon. Then the journey would reach its end.

It was an age-old dream in modern guise. This Promised Land went by many names at different times to a variety of people. Albion was the name usually given by the Paradise People. They believed they had found it. They were told they had found it. Then that dream faded, only to be rekindled by the desperate longing for somewhere, anywhere that might offer them Albion at last.

I thought of Simpson's story about a woman singing that trite, old song with its tango rhythm and its banal romance:

> *Si, si, señor,*
> *I'm waiting for*
> *You to adore*
> *Me with your charms.*
>
> *I will be true*
> *To loving you.*
> *What would I do*
> *Held in your arms?*

Once, years before, it had been very popular. It was a song heard all the time on the radio. That was before we born. There came a time when such songs faded, and *Si, Si Señor* was heard no more until it was used, ironically, as a theme to a nostalgic T.V. series. With another layer of irony the song became familiar again. So the old woman sang it as a fond memory of a dream that long ago she had shared with a million other women.

Geoffrey Heptonstall

Three

When I first met Rissa I told her a story. I wanted to tell her something of my childhood, something of my origins, something of me. How people react to such a story says a great deal about the way they feel about me. Rissa responded well. That was a good sign. She suggested at once we go riding together. I hardly knew her, and yet she was inviting me to share something with her. It was something important to her. She made it clear she loved horses.

She was a country girl, brought up in a village not far from the city, but far enough to feel distinct. It was another place, a quiet village where nothing happened and nothing was expected to happen. That had been her life entirely. She had gone to the village school, taken part in village activities with her mother, a farm secretary, and her father, a vet.

There was a girls' school in the next village. There Rissa went when she was twelve. The aim was to make a lady of her. 'So they failed there,' she said with conscious irony. She could no more shake off her superior manner than any of us could shake off the curse of our class. But, like me, Rissa was uneasy about the world and its injustice.

Neither of us knew how to apply a remedy to the ills of society. We walked along peaceable, privileged streets. We pursued peaceable, privileged interests about which we felt a guilt that was relieved but not eradicated by good works.

There was a sneering look in the faces of the Paradise People. That we could deal with. Malcontents who despise society despise even those attempting to improve society. 'The system's breaking down,' was the phrase Rissa heard when she went down to the riverside camp. It was a phrase from the Angel Tavern, an angry phrase from minds sent mad by the horrors of society. There was much to be tempted into anger about. But Rissa and I believed that art could create something more than illusions.

One evening we stood in the foyer of the theatre where Rissa worked. It was a serious play, a major work of Ibsen's familiar to a lot of A-level students because it was a set text. The sixth formers trouped in to the theatre, those embryonic professionals hoping to embark on a courses of study in medicine or law or architecture or teaching. It was amusing trying to decipher what each might be in a few years' time.

Some town girls passed, dressed up for a night out. In mocking mimicry of imagined superiority they shrieked, 'Oh, theeatah, haw, haw, haw!' That was how they saw theatre, something wholly apart from their lives, like Ascot and Glyndebourne and Cheltenham Ladies' College. It was for them within a social experience alien to all they knew. They would see the film of the play, but never the play itself. That was how their lives were limited. They were limited in ways neither Rissa nor I knew how to combat. We had no way of reaching those girls, no way of telling them that theatre might enrich their lives by widening the scope of their possibilities, by deepening their responses to the world. Save your breath; how would they listen?

The audience greatly appreciated the Ibsen play. It starred a couple of famous names who were ensuring the tour would conclude in the West End where visitors to London would marvel at such good theatre. Meanwhile the girls and their boys would grow in to women and men who think that certain good experiences are denied them. These thoughts haunted me.

We had met at the theatre. I saw her talking to other members of staff at the interval. So I knew she worked there, or was closely connected to the theatre. After the interval, returning to my seat I saw that she was sitting a few rows in front. She was young, alert and intelligent. The way her body curved as she sat appealed to me. She slid slowly and graciously into her seat, smoothing down her clothes with naturally sensual gestures that to me were the essentially feminine.

I was interested of course. Dormant feelings revived in me, not in paroxysms of desire, but in a gentle awakening that transformed into passion when I saw her again. This was a few days later. One afternoon I drove by theatre slowly in the frustrating trail of traffic that crawled through the city. Rissa hurried into the theatre by the stage door. So she did work there. I knew where she could be found without any clue about her name. This launched my mind into schemes of how I might discover her. Surely it would not be difficult?

In the end it was easier than I had dared imagine

possible. In the end she told me when we met in the street. It was as absurdly simple as that thanks to an accident, not a serious one, of the kind really does not happen except when it happens which is rarely if ever.

Maturity had not made me any more confident in speaking to women I liked. I have never been able to pick up women unknown to me. I lacked confidence in youth, like many young men. More mature now, my failed marriage shook me even though I was as responsible as Caroline for its failure. After the separation came the loneliness and the inevitable moments of desperation. I could dream of escort girls, but I had no intention of hiring one, not even for an evening's company that need not lead to a night in hotel room. I simply could not do it.

I longed for human contact, more specifically for female company. I was not desperate for sex with any available woman. For a long time I wanted Caroline, although I did not want her to come back to me. It had to end. And yet there remained that trace of her within me that would not die. You may say – I'm sure you're going to – that I didn't wish for Caroline to fade entirely.

The problem was in meeting someone else. It is never profitable to seek a variant on a theme. I didn't seek another Caroline. It seemed in our drifting part that her unsuitability was more evident than anything else. We had become bored with each other. No fresh start was going to change that fundamental truth of our relationship. We had grown up and in doing so had grown apart.

When it ceased to matter so much I was able to think about love again. Then I saw Rissa. There was an age gap, although it wasn't too great. It was easily bridgeable, I hoped. I wished. And so it was. She was mature. I remained quite young. In time we barely noticed the years. It wasn't too late for me start again, to fall in love almost as if for the first time, to feel the special sense of someone close to me.

'I stopped being Clarissa when I left home. It's so stunningly affected a name – if a name can be affected, which I suppose it can.' She said that at our first meeting to account for her curious name. 'Some people say Rissie, but I don't like that nearly as much.'

As we spoke I listened to her as I had not listened to anyone in a long time. I wasn't thinking other thoughts, nor did I wish to be anywhere else. My attention was fixed on Rissa alone.

How different she was to other women. Or so it seemed to me. That, of course, was the foundation of love. My desire for her stressed the agility and grace of her body in motion. I was captivated by her adornments – the sheen of her tights, the elegance of her silk scarf, the way her hair fell in sculpted waves, her smile, her scent of roses. But above any impulse to take hold and discover what pleasure and delight lay within was the need to know the self that bore her name.

The exploration began simply when in the street one day she passed by, only to slip and fall behind me. I looked round to see her holding onto a lamp post, like a drunk in a comedy sketch. The heel of her shoe had broken in the fall. 'This is too bloody awful,' she said. I saw the awkwardness of her position, and I could sense the embarrassment passing through her.

My car was very close by. I offered her a lift. Her first thought was to refuse. But her second thought was of hobbling down the street to a shoe shop. In London she might have hailed a cab. In Bath she had little choice, although she did refuse at first. 'Please,' I said. 'There's nothing round here.' I judged the tone of voice so perfectly that it reassured her as I had hoped. 'I can't think what else to do,' I added as if it were problem not hers. I had presumed a sympathy to which I had no right, but my presumption sounded so natural that it was disarming. Rissa's instinctive caution was surrendering.

When I came to know her I understood how, open as she was, she was careful with strangers. Once she knew me she revealed much without the least fear. It didn't take her long to know me. She judged people well, far more perceptively than I could summon. She read them at once, and unerringly.

I told her I was one of the people at Aventurine. 'That's where I've seen you,' she said. I told her I'd seen her at the theatre. 'Well,' Rissa said, 'we almost know each other.' We shook hands and exchanged names as I opened the car door for her.

I drove her to the theatre where, she said, she had another pair of shoes. 'I don't work all day in these.' She told me worked as publicity officer. It was interesting work she thoroughly enjoyed.

Her salary could not have bought her the clothes she wore. There was an air about her of money unearned. I was not sure at first how much substance was there. An impression given may be no more than a careful construct. Rissa dressed well. That was all I knew. I wondered how much theatre there was inside Rissa.

I was soon to learn there was very little. Her confidence enabled her to be open without making herself vulnerable. She was no more than acquaintance when she spoke in the frank, laconic terms, and its well-modulated tone, that marked her as different and, to me at least, very appealing. We had arranged to meet for a drink at The Garrick where photographs, many signed, of the actors at the theatre decorated the walls. It was quiet mid-evening, once the show had begun.

'It's a great place to work, and I love theatre, but I need family help to get by. I suppose I'm a bit of a daddy's girl. I expect you're quite close to your family? Of course you are. Well, then, we'll have the potential to get along very well.'

She had no intention of telling me where she lived that evening. Of course not, as Rissa would have said. A few days later we learned that we were almost neighbours. My small flat was near her small flat. We lived in the remnants of Palladian splendour that gave an air of grandeur to what was modest living. We both dreamed of something more. I didn't tell her at first that once I had had more. I thought it best to concentrate on the present, especially on my growing feelings for her.

The past was receding fast. It was becoming memory. Memory tends to be vague and unreliable. And where it is sharp it yet remains memory. My active feelings were moving forward. They were moving towards Rissa.

Quite how I felt about her it was too early to say. I barely knew her, although what I knew I liked. She was an easy person to know. I suspected that some people didn't like her precisely because she was so bright and direct. Some men may have liked the look of her without liking the challenge she presented. She had no intention of bolstering the fragile male ego, nor was she a bitch. She had a good heart. And she was nobody's fool. There was a crisp, clear air about her that I found so refreshing.

Four

One day when I was in the gallery two people came in who intrigued me by not looking like potential customers. They were too dishevelled and confused to be anything but hopeless drifters. I knew they had no interest in art. But they were looking for something. The location – it was on Pulteney Bridge – attracted them, as it attracted many people.

They wanted to talk to me. Without knowing me, without caring about the gallery, they wanted to speak because the gallery was there. That was how I met Mick and Trish. They told me of their plans. They were thinking of a better future for themselves.

'What was that place called? Oh yeah: Melbury Hall,' said Mick. I was surprised indeed to hear the name from his lips. 'You heard of a place called Melbury Hall?' Mick asked me.

'Yes, I know Melbury,' I said, hoping my reply would encourage Mick to say more.

But all Mick did was grunt. It was left to Trish to explain that they wanted to go there. 'Obvious we want to go there, Trish.'

'You want to know where it is?' I suggested.

'Yeah. Sort of.'

I told them where it was, and that it was remote. There was no bus to Combe Melbury. It was the sort of place where people with money went to escape urban living. It was a place to retire to, or to weekend in.

'We want to go there,' Trish said. 'There's opportunities.'

'It's a small village,' I insisted.

'Tell him, Mick.'

'I said shut it. I don't every fucker knowing what's happening.'

'We can trust him,' Trish said

'Can we? Can we trust you? How do we know?'

'How do we know?' Mick demanded.

'He's all right, aren't you?' Trish said. 'We know him.' Then to me she said, 'Can't stop our Mick once he gets started. I tell you. So we're going to that place.'

'Why don't you explain?' I asked.

'Because we don't want people knowing,' Mick replied. 'I asked you cause I wanted to know where it is. That's all. You don't need to know no more. The less you know the better for your own safety.'

'I'm not going anywhere bloody near Bradcombe, I'll tell you now,' Trish said. 'Not after what they done to me, the bastards. It was when I had my blackouts. Mick don't believe me, but, honest I tell you it were real bad, it were.'

'Trish, just shut it. I keep telling you that it's not that kind of place. It's a house that's all, a big, empty, old place. It'll be ours. I mean, not just you and me, but everyone who's there.'

'Well you told him now.'

'What if I have? I said I'll decide what's to be said and what's not to be said.'

I guessed, correctly, that they were planning to live

there – not with Dave Marsh's permission, of course. This was to be a squat. I guessed that Trish and Mick were accustomed to occupations. They lived an unofficial life. And who could blame them? They had no money in the chaos of their life together. They lacked the skills they needed to thrive in society. The best they could do was to survive in the underground that society ignores or fears. A chance to live in the country, to live in the dusty echoes of splendour had proved irresistible. They were going to walk to Combe Melbury.

'Is it far?' they asked, having no idea of distance and time. I told them it was a long way. Trish assured me they were accustomed to walking. They had walked from somewhere – she had forgotten where. The journey had taken the two of them days. They had lost count of the days. The walk to Combe Melbury was going to take all day and more. I pictured the two of them at a crossroads somewhere beyond Radstock, sore of foot, hungry, thirsty and uncertain of where to go. No car would stop for them. They would have no money for a bus that could take them part of the way. It was too late to turn back. Each was sure to blame the other.

It was not entirely selfless of me to offer to take them. When I said I was going most of the way I was speaking the truth. But my offer to drive Trish and Mick to Combe Melbury was slightly mischievous, I cannot deny. Dave Marsh's last words to me continued to sting in my memory. I ought to have risen above such thoughts. The temptation to do Marsh a mild disservice was too much for me. Yes, it was wrong of me. I pretended to myself that I wasn't getting back at Marsh, although I knew I was.

That last meeting had vexed me. Dave Marsh had changed. He was harder than the genial buffoon I had known before. His eyes were colder, his voice sharper. I could no longer think of him as a friend.

And so I helped Trish and Mick load their belongings into my car. 'We'll be there in no time,' I assured them. 'You'll like Melbury. Sometimes it's good to get out of town even so lovely a town as this.'

'I'm not going anywhere near Bradcombe,' Trish said. 'I hate there. What they done to me there was not Christian. They're heathens in that place.'

'If you was in Bradcombe that proves you're mental,' Mick retorted unhelpfully.

I assured Trish that we were going nowhere near Bradcombe, with its hospital. I thought of that forbidding Victorian asylum. There were bars on the window, like a prison. No-one likes to think of the treatment of the inmates there. But that it was in times less enlightened than ours. Surely nothing like that would happen now? My knowledge of mental heath interventions was vague. Drugs and shock treatment could be misapplied. Imagine the scene where Trish is held down, screaming, kicking, cursing. That would be her in Bradcombe. Something had to be done to calm her. Who is to say for sure what was done, and whether it was right that it should have been done?

'It was what them so-called expert doctors did what they did to me. Interfering bastards. Perverts.' Trish continued her complaint.

'You never told us that, Trish,' Mick said. 'You never told us they was perverts in there.'

'I did tell you, Mick. So get your bloody facts right. I did fuckin' tell you. Only you wasn't listening. I have been fucked about by the whole fuckin' lot of them.'

'Shame you got madness in you, Trish.'

'I haven't no more. No more I have got madness in me. Get your bloody facts right, Mick, before you start your accusings of others. Typical of you to say something you know fuck-all about. You was always like that ever since I've known you. Saying this and that, and thinking you're the big clever. Like when you said that about that song whatever it were. And it weren't him that sung it at all, like I said. I'll never forget that. You still owe me the money for that. You see. You see, you don't know everything as much as you think you do, Mr. Clevershit.'

We were not out of the city. I could see that there was a price to be paid for offering those two a lift. I suggested we listen to some music, but all my possibilities were sullenly rejected by Mick. Trish said nothing except, 'I really like that song by whatever-he's-called. You know – that one I really like. Dead good, that song.'

There was a sign on the road for Bristol. We were not taking that road, but forking left at The Globe Inn through Corston and Marksbury. 'Shit pub, that,' Mick said of The Globe. 'Went in there once. Better pubs in Bristol. Bristol's all right for pubs. Fuck-all else there, though.'

'I met Frigger in Bristol,' Trish said. 'He was all right. Do you know Pennard Street? There's a pub there where I just didn't know what I were doing in the back room. It was Frigger who give me them pills. Right out of it, I was. Funny how these things happen. You know how they just happen? Frigger was all right. He treated me O.K., anyway. Say what you like about them, but he was all right. Like, if I got out of my head or anything, Frigger would get me home in a taxi. What I call a gentleman. Someone who knows how to treat a girl correct.'

'Which pub was it, then?' Mick asked.

'I bleedin' telled you, Mick. Don't you listen? It were Pennard Street or something.'

'Right. Well, which one?'

'How should I know, Mick? I was out of my head on pills that night.'

'Don't talk stupid.'

'Who's talking stupid? It's you who's stupid. Talking stupid.'

'It's not me who's fuckin' mental.'

'Excuse me, but I am not mental no more. You're a bastard, you are, Mick.'

'No, they was married before they had me.'

'You hurt me, you pig. Last time, you hurt me. Do you know that?' At this point Trish began to cry.

'Trouble with you, Trish, is you never fuckin' listen. Shame about you, really. 'Cause it's not your fault. Well, I mean, it is your fault. But you can't help it, like. Shame.' This did nothing to relieve the hurt. Trish cried to herself while Mick started to hum a tune, beating time with his hands. It was a while before he tried to make amends. 'Thing is, Trish, we're both victims of a society that does not give a toss about the rights of free-born Englishmen. That's us, Trish, you and me. We are the English race. Born to rule the world, we are.'

I suggested we stop somewhere along the way for coffee. This I was determined to do, for the atmosphere in the car was intolerable. This was how they lived their lives. It was such an oppressive existence. There seemed no escape from the relentless attrition of their relationship.

Yes, I could pretend it was a dream. But this was very real. The hope was that they would change their minds about Melbury Hall. Gladly then should I have given them the bus fare back to town. But there was no hint of any change of plan. They intended to remain with me all the way to Combe Melbury. They were happy to do so, for they were never happy about anything. They had disturbingly intense feelings that they were matters of instinct. I dared not trust them. I wanted rid of them. I judged it would be perhaps another half hour before we reached Combe Melbury on these country roads. We were half way there in the longest hour I have ever known.

'I suppose it'll be all nice and country,' Trish said in the roadside café. 'I like the country even if it is a bit scary at night. Yeah, we'll be O.K. there – better than some of the holes we've lived. Holes that he's found for us. I don't why I put up with him, to be quite honest and frank with you. Thing is when you're with someone you sort of can't imagine how it's going to be if you wasn't with him.'

'Shall I tell you what she done the last place we were?' Mick said.

'You don't listen to him. He doesn't know.'

'Shows how mental she is. She only goes and stands on the table before pulls down...'

'That is not true. I never done what you said. I never done nothing like that ever. It's typical of him. That is not true. This is what it's like for me.'

'I wouldn't be with her if I had money. If I had money I'd have posh women. I wouldn't marry any, though. I'd only marry in my own class. That way I'd know what I was getting.'

'I don't think marriage is good idea because of what my dad did to our mother and me.'

'He didn't do nothing to you, Trish. Nothing that did you bad. I mean, you got to have it sometime.'

'Yeah. And it hurt me. Think about that, Mick.'

'It always hurts a bit to begin with. Fact of life. Thing is, the way I see it, better it was your dad than some stranger doing it to you. Anyway, I'm sick of hearing about you Trish. I know you can't help it, but I'm sick of it all the same. They should've kept you in, I think. Either that or fuck some sense into you.'

'I think we need to move on,' I suggested with an evenness of temper that astonished me.

'I swear to God,' Trish said, 'I will leave him one of these days. I don't need nobody – nobody like him, anyway. Trouble is all men are the same. I mean, you're not, but that's cause you're all pansy – no offence. But, I mean, you got feelings.'

'I got feelings,' Mick rejoined. 'And that's why you get on my fuckin' nerves.' Turning to me he added, 'She'll be up Bristol again soon. You just see. It's all she knows. Well, it's easy money.'

'You got no right,' Trish shouted. 'You got no right to say that. I was not doing it except as a favour to Frigger, which makes it a lot of different from what you're making it out. So get your bleedin' facts right before you start slagging me off in front of everybody.'

'I never said nothing,' making his way to the washrooms.

There was a silence while Trish dried her eyes, and composed herself. Away from Mick, she was able to do quite quickly. 'Mick i'n't so bad,' Trish attempted to explain. 'He can be a good laugh sometimes. And he looks after me better than Frigger. I say about Frigger, but, to be honest, Mick doesn't make me do what Frigger did. I suppose I'd like to meet a real gentleman.'

Trish glanced for a second at me. I looked away to see Mick returning. It was time to go. Mick, however sat down again.

'She been mental again?'

'Excuse me, Michael Gibson, but I was having what I calls a very polite and quite interesting conversation, as a matter of fact, with this gentleman who has been kind enough to offer us a ride to where we're going – which is very nice of him, in my opinion... And if you can't behave decent and proper I suggest you shut your effin' lip.'

There was a mist over Sedgemoor as we came down from the Mendip Hills. The high tor of Glastonbury with its tower at the crown had a primeval look, as it often did. Sedgemoor could be inexplicably strange at times. People lived ordinary lives here, sometimes surprisingly mundane in a routine of work and leisure that knew about material things. That ordinariness did nothing to alleviate the strangeness that could sequester this isolated world.

'Britain,' Mick pronounced after a mercifully long silence. 'Look at it. This is the country we fight wars for. This is the country that Socialism cannot destroy. Ever. Socialism has come into this country again, right, but it cannot destroy us. And that is because of our empire. The British Empire is important because, I'll tell you why, that wherever you work it's the Englishman who gets the best jobs and the best wages. The British Empire teaches the world to respect what our country is and always fuckin' will be. I was in Africa, and the bosses was each a white Englishman. I know because I was there. I had good wages. I had heathens doing as I said. Useless bastards they were an' all.'

'They say darkies stink when they sweat,' Trish responded.' I wouldn't want to be out Africa way. They say darkies stink. When I were in hospital there were this fella, dark, who...'

'Women stink sometimes,' Mick muttered.

It was almost the last thing I remember Mick saying. I don't recall him thanking me for the lift. The truth was (although neither understood this until it was too late) that I dropped them two or three miles away. I let them think that West Melton was their destination. It was deceitful of me, I knew, but enough of them was enough. I hoped never to see them again.

'Can't be worse than where was, Trish,' Mick remarked at the roadside. Trish tried to kiss me by way of thanks. I avoid that, but wished her well. I felt pity for her in her life of confusion and pain. I could not imagine the future for her. I supposed she was going to be the same in another five or ten years.

I tried not to imagine the mess they would make of Melbury Hall. I hoped that it would not be too serious. The place was very likely in a state of disrepair already. Some time of neglect would have taken its toll. There may not have been a great deal more that the squatters could do to make it worse. That, at least, is what I hoped. It was a way of salving my conscience.

I had no-one to blame but myself. No pressure of any kind had forced me to do this. I had no motive beyond a little mischief, and even that was not intense. I had supposed it to be harmless. I simply wanted to annoy Dave Marsh. I had no dark thoughts of revenge. I wished him no serious harm. I simply hoped he would be inconvenienced. Another man was his enemy, not I.

Five

Imagine the scene:

The step on the stair was faltering. One foot had a heavier tread. The rhythm was unmistakable. Someone lame was approaching with measured step born of his affliction, like a soldier. He could easily have been mistaken for a soldier with his commanding demeanour on a slender frame. The visitor's face was alert, a little cautious but composed. Like the tread upon the stair, it was a purposeful countenance.

At the landing the visitor smiled politely without speaking. The fine old clock struck eleven. The visitor was exceptionally punctual.

Standing in the doorway of his office was Dave Marsh, adjusting his cuffs and shirt collar in anticipation of the visitor. This was a visit to which Marsh clearly attached some importance.

Jackie took the visitor's coat. 'But I'm forgetting my manners,' Marsh said, shaking the visitor's hand, and offering him a chair. 'Some coffee, Jackie, I think. And we'll not want to be disturbed.'

Jackie went out to make the coffee. The visitor sat the other side of Marsh's desk. He was a young man, dressed smartly in fashionable and expensive clothes that achieved an air of casual prosperity that was so artfully displayed. He was perhaps something in a creative sphere, or possibly in academic life. It was very likely the young man lived in a combination of the two, and that he was successful at whatever he was doing.

'Yes, I heard that you were back,' Marsh said. 'Good to see you again.' In Marsh's personal papers somewhere in the elegant nineteenth century bureau with its walnut veneer was the letter that he had trembled, recognizing the handwriting of someone he thought had gone for ever. It had been along time since he had heard anything of his old friend.

At first Marsh was deeply alarmed to see that this ghost was in contact, and further that he hoped to see Marsh again. But his old friend had written of his forgiveness. He accepted what had happened. He gave Marsh and Gelina his blessing.

Life had changed for Simpson also. Much had happened, beginning with his slow recovery in the care of his family. He had travelled, all the while reading and thinking, reflecting on his past, and on how the course of his life might develop.

In a short time Simpson had found all the things he wanted. He bore Marsh no ill-will. He bore no-one any grudges. He had no regrets. The misfortunes, he concluded, were largely his own fault. He had misjudged life. Of course that had been some time ago. He would not make such mistakes again.

Marsh was relieved to hear it. His life had been transformed, and now he was a happy man. He didn't want any lingering ill-feeling to cloud his days. He had known enough bitterness and misery to understand its destructive power. It was better to forgive and, where possible, to forget. Simpson, he thought, always had been wiser than his years. Where other young, or not so young, men would be spiteful and vengeful, Simpson was being sensible and kind. Marsh couldn't help but admire him, and feel rather ashamed. He felt ashamed not of what he had done (that was in the past, after all), but of a wronged man's generosity to him. Quite saintly, when you thought about it.

'Well, I'm glad you see it that way,' Marsh said. 'Water under the bridge. What do these things matter, after all, when you think of the state of the world. We should count our blessings.'

'It was time for me to move on,' Simpson said. 'I see that now.'

'Exactly. There's a time and a place for everything. Some things are just meant to be, and I feel Evangel...'

'Dave, there's something else I want to say. I don't know how to put this...'

'No need, young man. I think I understand. When you've lived as long as I have you learn a thing or two. It's the ones who don't learn I've no sympathy for. Life is about experience. You gain something from experience that they'll not teach you in school. It's something nobody can teach you. It's called life. Once you've a bit of experience under your belt, as I know you have, you get to see things as they really are, as I see you have. In this life we all have choices. Choose wisely and you'll not go wrong. Mind you, there's a few mistakes to be made along the way before you can start making the right choices. No question about that.'

At this point perhaps Jackie politely knocked on the

door to bring in the coffee. The tresses of her hair feel as carefully she leaned over to place the tray on Marsh's desk. Her clothes allowance was evidently generous. in immaculate skirt and smooth, glistening tights she played her part perfectly. Sweetly she smiled at the visitor, as she smiled at every visitor. She knew what men were thinking. They always thought that. But modestly Jackie took her leave of the two men, leaving them to their business of which she knew nothing.

Jackie had risen early, taking so much time in preparation for the day. She would spend her day performing her tasks both eagerly and efficiently. Encompassing her would be unfailing courtesy and flawless good humour. She very likely would work late without thought of extra pay. And then she would go home with aching feet and tired eyes. No man considered that.

'Lovely girl,' Marsh said when the men were alone again. 'There's not many like her. Hard-working, loyal – not like your average British worker. If everyone was like Jackie we'd still be a nation that counted in the world. We'd be able to hold our heads up high instead of shuffling along. Look at people today. They look like they've just been released into the community.'

Then there would be silence as the two men sipped at their coffee. Neither perhaps knew quite what to say next. There were things to be said, of course. Simpson had come to tell Marsh he forgave him for the betrayal. He clearly had another motive. There was more he wanted to say. Marsh guessed that it was a business proposition. Simpson had some scheme in mind for which he needed Marsh's help. It may have been a question of finance, but, Marsh believed, it was more likely to be the wealth of Marsh's experience.

The wealth of experience – it was a phrase Marsh loved to turn over in his mind in moments of contemplation.

Dave Marsh once told Caroline and me a story. No doubt he told it to Simpson at some stage. It was a sad, painful childhood memory. As he told it he went back into childhood. He was back in the village schoolroom thirty and more years before:

'You know, I've always wanted to be able to fly. Like, when I was a boy I had this dream I could fly. You know how kids have dreams. In my dream I was walking down a staircase when suddenly and naturally somehow I flew. I could fly. I could bloody well fly. Floating through the air, like a leaf I once saw caught by a wave so that it rose higher and higher. I thought of it as a... as an angel. And that's who I was. For a moment, in my sleep, I was an angel.

'Well, I decided I write about it. The next time we had composition at school I wrote about my dream. This was my golden moment. I was never good at writing. Never good at anything in school, really. But this was to be my golden moment. I'd never been in a plane but I knew what it was like to fly.

'You know what happened? What happened? You want to know what? Nothing. That is what. And worse than nothing. They shot me down. I hit the ground at maximum velocity. Wham!

'It had been my golden moment. My beautiful dream. They crushed it, like they crushed the butterflies they caught in the schoolyard. They laughed. The little bastards laughed, the girls included. They all tore at me with their silly bloody fuckin' laughter. Ha, ha, ha. Ha, ha, ha. The worst sound I have ever heard in my ears. Ha, ha, ha. But not one of them could have written like I wrote that afternoon. Not one ever did nearly as best a piece of writing. Not any of them did nothing as that composition of mine. That's what I said. I said, "What does any of you do that's so good? Biggest half of you be stupider than anything."

'It was true, but it did me no good. No good. You know why? Because from that day on I gave up. I didn't bother. There were exams. I failed them, of course. I might have got through if it hadn't have been for that afternoon. Not that I was ever the brightest of kids. I had a chance, though, before. Not after. Never after. I sort of fell behind. Bottom of the class. The dunce. I acted the clown. I acted the fool. It was the only way to stop them. Making them laugh at me was like my way of fending off the hurt. I was saying, "Go on – laugh some more at me. If you laugh at me you won't hit me." That's what I hated – the ragging, the chivvying. The kicks, the smacks. Day after day.

'It was him who started it, the teacher. Mr. Evans. He was the first to laugh. I handed in my composition, and he laughed. He pissed his self. I couldn't believe it. When I'd expected a gold star I got nothing except a load of corrections in red ink. And the comment on the bottom of the page: *A silly idea, sloppily expressed, and untidily presented. The worst composition it has ever been my misfortune to read.* I kept it, though. I kept it like I've kept nothing else. I still have it somewhere I expect. My golden moment.'

It had taken Marsh a long time to find his next golden moment. The sadness was that he had robbed a young man of his moment. But, Marsh reasoned, Simpson was young. There would be other times in the future, whereas Gelina was Marsh's last chance. That was the difference. Who could have blamed Marsh for taking that chance?

'So,' Marsh said, 'you've something you want to say to me, young man?'

'Dave,' Simpson began, 'I had time to think when I was recovering. I thought of a lot of things. Silly things. Important things. But I had time to really look at my future. I realized I needed to find new ground. I'd known ever since I climbed up from Paradise Park. But when I had real time to think I knew where I was going.'

Simpson paused. He held that paused for a while. Finally Marsh took his cue, 'And where was that, young man?'

'California.'

'I'm going there myself in a day or two. It'll be my first visit out west. I liked New York, I have to say. Like London on stilts, you might say. I dare say I'll like California, too. Evangelina's there. Doing so well.'

'Yes, Dave, I know. I saw some of her work in a Santa Monica gallery.'

'Well, she's designing for Universal now.'

'Yes, Dave, I know. I heard.'

The air in the room was changing. It was growing colder. It was a chill that Marsh feared. There was some bad news coming. How bad he couldn't judge so soon. He needed to hear more, although he had no wish to hear more.

'Dave, I have something to tell you. I don't know how to put this.'

'Has something happened? Tell me what's happened? Have you seen her? Have you spoken to Evangelina?'

'No, Dave, I've not spoken to her. I've not seen her.'

'Thank God for that,' Marsh said, relieved. 'For a moment I thought....Never mind what I thought. I'm just glad nothing's happened. You had me worried for a minute there, young man. If anything were to happen...'

Simpson pulled out a large envelope from his document case. 'I've not seen Gelina. I never want to see her again. You understand why. I came here to tell you that I don't care anymore. If the two of you are happy it's no concern of mine. I don't care, Dave. You don't think I can be bothered with either of you now.'

'Then why did you come here?' Marsh asked, rising from his chair to indicate the conversation was over.

Simpson began opening the envelope. 'I've not seen Gelina. But I know someone who has. He's told me all about it.' And then he placed several photographs of Gelina in a Beverly Hills hotel room with another man.

The photographs spoke for themselves, enabling Simpson to leave without another word said. Dave Marsh, as one would expect, was void of all response. He simply stared at the photographs.

Perhaps his first thought was that they were clever fakes. He scrutinized them to be sure that it really was his young bride on that bed. Was it possible that her face had been superimposed on some tart's body? It was possible, but he knew it wasn't the case. This was his beloved wife, the artist Evangelina Marsh, performing intimately with some ageing American who was rich, powerful and open to persuasion at a price.

That lingerie – she had worn it for Marsh. He had bought it for her among the many gifts he had lavished on her. She had worn those things when she gave Marsh the exclusive pleasure that now she was prepared to offer to a stranger.

Her justification would be that it was only one time. Seduced by the glamour of Hollywood, alone and young and vulnerable, she was easy prey for some slick tycoon who knew all the angles.

Gelina would beg Marsh for his forgiveness. But the golden moment had gone for ever. How could things be the same? Whether it was one man or a hundred the threads were broken. Marsh was going to be haunted by those photographs for the remaining years of his life, long years he would face in the twilight. Nothing was ever going to be golden again.

Imagine the scene as Dave Marsh left his office hurriedly, in a daze, out to seek the oblivion that was his only consolation now. The photographs he left for Jackie to find. That was how, some time later and by chance, I learned what sent Dave Marsh mad.

Did I feel any sympathy for him? I did. It was a mean thing that Simpson did. I cannot say it was no more than Marsh deserved. I feel that it was too terrible an act of revenge, for it was sure to crush him, if not to destroy him.

Of course anyone could see that Gelina was going to fly away. A part of her had gone already. It was never a serious marriage, surely? Whatever happened Marsh was going to be hurt. But to be wounded as he was with such a thrust of the dagger – that was so cruel. It made my little act of mischief seem nothing. I was shamed of delivering Trish and Mick to Melbury. I doubted, though, that Simpson felt the least sense of guilt over what he had done. I doubted that because Marsh had made himself open to such revenge.

The betrayer must always fear betrayal shall be his fate. It was the same story as ever: Dave Marsh forgot that other people had desires as strong as his own.

Three:

Sunrise

104

One

'I ought to be called Vivien Devine. Then, maybe, I'd have a future in Hollywood.' Nerys laughed at the absurdity of her good fortune. Hollywood was Hollywood. It was a well-deserved break after years of valiantly trying to make ends meet in England. We were so pleased for her. Rissa had known Nerys ever since Nerys had appeared in a bad but popular thriller which transferred to the West End. That had brought her to the attention of television. And from there came the call to Burbank.

Dreams of Shakespeare lingered. They need not be abandoned, she said. American television was going a number of debts. With money, she said, much more was possible.

No, she didn't think that Hollywood meant super-stardom. She was sensible enough to know how many people there were in a few square miles of aspiration and desperation. A t.v. series wanted 'an English girl'. That, Nerys knew, was all. The pay of course exceeded her hopes. And it was going to raise her profile for a time. After that there was no telling.

I was struck by something that sad woman Trish said on the journey to Combe Melbury: 'I like dreams. I dream all sorts. Better than life, really.' It was true that her life was a hopeless tangle she could never sort out. It was easy to see why she preferred her dreams.

Trish and Mick spent their life confusing dreams

with reality. Melbury Hall for them was a dream. Once they were everything would come together. Life's confusions would disentangle themselves in an instant miracle of bliss.

It was the same feeling for Dave Marsh. He also believed that Melbury Hall was going to be the solution. Once there he would discover all those things that had evaded him over the years. He had thought Simpson could provide one kind of answer. He had thought Gelina could provide another. He had been betrayed, needlessly, wantonly and mindlessly betrayed. But once he was secure inside Melbury Hall, once his plans, whatever they were, came to fruition there would be no more bewilderment, no more frustration, no more striving, no more disappointment. The dream would fulfil its promise.

The consolations were there for all those who had found life had not lived up to expectations. The consolations were there for all of us, to a greater or lesser degree. Rissa and I wanted to see *Eustace* when it reached our screens, and not only because someone we knew was going to be in it. We liked Hal Schneider, taking the title role of the loveable schmuck who somehow wins in the end. We could laugh at *Eustace* in his pratfalls. We were going to laugh at him. And we were going to laugh with him. There was every chance that *Eustace* would be a big hit.

The hope for Nerys was something more would come of it. We thought her to be capable as an actress, with the potential of reaching something substantial.

We tried imagining suitable roles for her in plays that would stretch her and thereby bring out the best in her.

We promised that we would go out to the West Coast to see her. It was a promise we intended to keep. One of the last things we said was that we hoped she wouldn't come across Gelina Marsh. It was, the three of us decided, unlikely. In a metropolis the chances of meeting were slim. And yet each of us privately thought of the chance encounters we had had. I certainly had seen people by chance so often.

Inevitably, Nerys did come across Gelina. When Gelina's work for Universal finished other studios wanted her. The offer she took meant that an eventual meeting with Nerys was very likely.

It was Nerys who first suggested Gelina might design for the stage. At her first Aventurine exhibition Nerys, unknown to me then, came along to the preview. To her subsequent regret she found Gelina sufficiently engaging, as well as talented, to make that suggestion. Dave Marsh, of course, noted what said. It was his influence that transformed a casual remark into a major commitment.

It wasn't Nerys's fault, although of course she blamed herself. She knew all about Gelina and the damage she had done to at least two lives. Nerys recognized her to be a dangerous predator.

Nerys had resolved that in any circumstance she was going to keep Gelina at arm's length. 'I'll be no more than polite. I'll have to be polite, but I don't have to be more than that,' she told us.

Our friend's heart sank when Gelina Marsh called. Nerys had no choice but to agree to meet up with her. She feared the power that Gelina might have. In Hollywood you have to be nice to everyone.

Fortunately for Nerys things turned out differently. Of course the exact details have to be imagined. I try to imagine the scene:

'The World's End', she suggested. 'Main Street. It's a really cool place. They have live music, you know. It's, like, good. Good wine. I mean, I especially recommend their merlot.' She was not American by birth. She had been resident in Santa Monica for not much longer than a year, but already she had acquired the familiarity with her new home to speak in the local way. Its cadences were hers. Its vocabulary was hers. The vowels, too, were shaping their course. She clearly had no intention now of going back. Sometimes she betrayed herself by trying a little too hard. But as time went by things were easier. Memories, in any case, were short. This was a nation accustomed to migration. Nobody cared about such things.

What mattered was success. Gelina Marsh was a success. This translated into money and the confidence that money generates. Gelina had never been poor. Her first, short-lived marriage in England had been to a rich man. He had enabled her to visit the West Coast many times before she decided to settle. It had been an inevitable decision, given the way Los Angeles had taken to her. She soaked up the adulation and, especially, the envy. Her dating of a rock guitarist made her a name that had nothing to do with her art, but everything to do with her ambitions.

When Gelina suggested that Nerys and she meet at the World's End was a good choice, given its ambience, and its location half way between Gelina's Santa Monica and the Nerys's beach apartment Venice. 'After that we can drive some place to eat. Whatever you want.'

They were going incognito. This suited the actress who was being spoken of as the up and coming are spoken of in Hollywood. Gelina, for her part, hoped that they would be recognized. The important about celebrity was to be noticed. Not be noticed was to be sent out to the desert to wait for a prolonged death of excruciating agony.

To be noticed one needed some skill in the art of desperately failing to be anonymous. Only if you are somebody do you need to seek anonymity. The trick was to behave so effacingly that one's whole being screamed 'Look at me!' without a syllable uttered or a glance exchanged.

And so they agreed to meet. At a little after seven-thirty Gelina parked her car on Ocean Park Boulevard. Looking neither to right nor left she hurried down the sidewalk to Main Street. Had she not recognized the voice from the shadows she wouldn't have stopped and turned and looked at him. He was someone she dared not ignore.

Simpson had a half smile playing on his lips as he took a couple of steps closer. 'I'm afraid Nerys couldn't make it,' he said. 'It looks as though it's just the two of us.'

'How did you know?' Gelina asked, giving Simpson the advantage he needed. He had shaken her confidence quite seriously.

'I beat the truth out of her,' he replied mockingly. Changing expression with chilling ease, he said more seriously, 'Hollywood is a village. At times the world is a village.'

Gelina did not wish to meet his glance. In her mind there was guilt, or fear, or both blended into shame. She had a conscience still about the hurt she had done Simpson. Her fear since then had been this moment.

'Look, I've nothing to say to you.'

'But, Gelina, darling, I've so much I want to say to you.'

'I am not listening to you. I am not listening. I do not want to know you, speak to you, or think about you.'

'The world listens to me,' Simpson replied with a calm that was more threatening than anger. 'Do you know how many people watch my show? All those millions who trust me: I am their guide, their mentor, their friends. I change lives. I change them for the better, whereas some people, like yourself, change for the worse.'

'I am not listening,' Gelina nervously insisted. 'Leave me now or I'll scream my head off.'

'Scream your head off here on Main Street. And be committed. It was so fortunate for the patient that a high-profile life therapist was on hand to help.' Simpson still did not change his expression. 'So you listen to what I have to say. There's a new world dawning. I can feel its vibrations as I walk along the shore. Even in a drug store I can feel the rhythms of change. It is there all time. I can feel it, and I want you to feel it, Gelina. I want you to feel what I feel.'

'Please go. Just leave me. Forget me. It's too late.'

'Interesting how dreams are real even when they don't come true,' Simpson continued. 'You remember how it was in the garden, in the summerhouse? We had a dream we wove together. It meant so much to me, but nothing to you.'

'That's not true. I was young. A rich, powerful man overwhelmed me with jewels and promises and all the things that drowned me in confusion. You got hurt, and I got hurt. And I've paid for what I did. I've let men use me. I don't blame Dave for wanting a divorce. I'm a slut, and I know it, and I don't want to be a Hollywood slut.'

Tears, heartfelt in their way, streamed down the face of a young woman whose ambition had led her to this melodrama. In the shadows of an evening everything was quiet but for the sound of two young people acting out their despair. They were acting so well it might have been real. Who knows?

They went somewhere a long Main Street, perhaps to Joe's Diner, an ordinary place, but a quiet one where they could talk as they needed to. Later they could drive to Beverly Hills and dine in some style. But for the moment they needed some place nearby where they could talk quietly.

What of know of Simpson suggests he reassured Gelina with honeyed words: 'Don't ever think about your-self, Gelina. You did what you felt was right. As long as you always were true to yourself there is no blame. You must not feel guilty. Guilt is such a negative feeling. It destroys the spirit. And you have such a beautiful spir-it, Gelina. I never doubted that. You didn't hurt. I did it to myself. When I fell it wasn't because of you.'

Then there was a pause. Simpson said nothing more. He didn't need to say anything further. It was Gelina who spoke, as Simpson anticipated she would speak. A look of pale dread came over her as she whis-pered, 'You mean he pushed you? Oh my....'

'I wasn't going to tell you, Gelina,' Simpson mur-mured, reaching his hand out to her. 'I didn't want you to know. I hoped you'd never guess. I didn't want you to know.'

Two

Imagine another scene.

He looked again at the secluded setting. There was no-one in view. He was sure of that. There was nothing out of place. It was a tranquil scene, a country idyll of a kind that he had dreamed would one day be his. From so unpromising a beginning in life he had come to this house in its grandeur. It was his, and all the land surrounding it in the combe. It would be his for as long as he lived. It would be his when he died and was buried in the village churchyard. This he had arranged so that when, after many years of gracious and pleasurable life here, he would settle into the very earth itself in peace, knowing that he had lived a good life. He was a man who loved life in all its variety. He loved his country on whose fecund ground he trod. This meadow, those trees, and the house itself – they were good. They were the England for which he was prepared to nurture and to defend.

Dave Marsh looked again. No, there was no-one. But there was something. It was a sound, a murmur in the distance. He heard it again. This time it was closer. Something was coming nearer. Then there was a shadow and the screeching of a bird. It seemed to give out a mocking cry. It was laughing, actually laughing, this dark predator from the depths of the wood.

Marsh looked up, his vision dazzled by the sunlight. He could make out the ominous presence of a raven hovering overhead with what seemed to be conscious menace. He felt under attack. He was sure the bird knew the fear it brought to his spirit. Marsh was truly afraid.

He stumbled, fell to his knees on the moist grass and muddied soil. When he looked up again it was at a clear, cloudless sky of a perfect morning in early summer. There was no raven. There was no shadow. There was no sound in the stillness that was itself strange. Even the sight of the house so close gave Marsh no sense of relief. He sensed menace, wholly unexpected and deeply disturbing. He was sure something was happening.

It was, to his alarm, something he could not control. Nature was out there, watching him. He was being judged. There was no human out there. Of that he was quite sure. There was nobody to harm him now. He was well protected. And in an urban space Dave Marsh would have felt wholly in control. Out here it was different. This was a world of which he was not master.

Marsh was wrong about not being seen. We could see him. We were watching from the trees. We saw the bird fly out from somewhere close by. We saw Dave Marsh's look of surprise turn to horror. We saw everything. I had seen Marsh stumble many times, but not when he was sober. These days he was more purposeful than ever, and less inclined to seek oblivion.

He had sought oblivion in those terrible days when he first learned of Gelina's infidelity. He had roared through life out of control by all accounts. It was said that at night he disappeared into the alleys of Bristol. Whether he was searching for consolation or a means of venting his anger no-one could say. Perhaps it was a fusion of the two that took him to those dark quarters.

Even by day he was seen drinking, often for hours on end. It was a customary sight to see him helplessly carried to a car. He was no longer a figure of harmless fun, but of pathos. His reputation was rapidly sliding. In business and in public life they were turning away, pretending not to hear, not to know.

A reputation is such a frail creature, easily lost in the cruel judgements of the world. Dave Marsh was set to lose everything. That was because he clearly did not care. He wanted to lose. He wanted the world to know how he felt. He felt shame, loss, humiliation and anger. So easily he thought he had gained everything. For a time he had. Now it was taken from him, snatched out of his hand when it was tantalizingly close.

But for an unlikely intervention there's no doubt that Dave Marsh would have gone under. Quite what happened no-one knew, not even Jackie, his loyal and sweet-natured assistant, who knew most things about Dave Marsh. She had covered for him as best she could. She had thoughts of ways she might seek help for him. But when someone is on a course as surely as Dave Marsh was there is not much assistance available.

It was as if one night in the gutter he looked up at the stars, and never looked back from that moment. It was not love that changed him. Of that I am quite certain. Someone spoke to him. Someone said something that changed his mind. Someone gave Marsh hope. Someone put an idea into his head. That idea was Melbury Hall.

What was happening there Jackie had no idea. It made her feel uneasy. She had accepted over the years Marsh in all his moods, and with all his failings. But this she could not accept. It was wrong, she said, although she had no clear idea what it was that was wrong.

Jackie felt so strongly that she sought work elsewhere, the excuse being that she needed to be near her ageing parents in Hampshire. And so she went, no longer felt needed. She had been indispensable, only to find herself excluded. She no longer mattered to Marsh. He was a man who had one thought only, whatever that thought was.

It had a location, and a name. Melbury Hall was the shell in which Dave Marsh's idea was taking shape. The nature of the idea was a matter of supposition. Jackie had felt uneasy about it, and so had I.

So uneasy had I felt that I turned down a very lucrative commission. I told Rosaline at the gallery, if only to prevent her hearing from Marsh himself. I wasn't sure how she was going to take the news. It happened that she agreed, partly because Rosaline trusted my judgement, and also because she felt (from all I had said and from what she had heard elsewhere) that Marsh was not entirely on the level.

'It's a cat house,' Rosaline said.

'You think so?'

'I know so. And so do you. But it's more than that, isn't it?'

'Rissa thinks the same.'

'Well, of course she does. I don't know why you're so reluctant to admit that Marsh is corrupt. The only question is what sort of funny business is he up to?'

I had more or less the same conversation with both Rosaline and Rissa. The women were unhesitatingly direct, unafraid of their common-sense intuitions. I was reluctant to consider what I didn't like to think. I was soft-pedalling perhaps because I knew Marsh. It was not that I felt any warmth toward him now. But because I knew of the way he was, and what he was capable, I dared not admit what the two women who meant, in their different ways, most to me spoke of so determinedly.

'He likes power,' Rosaline/Rissa concluded. 'And money. And the pleasures that money can give.'

'I know that,' I said defensively.

'Added to which, he's angry now. He's seriously angry.'

'But what can he do?'

Rosaline demurred from saying more. It was Rissa who said, 'Anger needs a focus. Marsh needs someone to blame.'

'That's Gelina of course,' I said.

'No, it isn't. If it were he'd be acting very differently. He's not setting a trap for her. This is about something else.'

'You make it sound very serious,' I said.

'It is serious.'

'How do you know?'

'Melbury Hall is hidden away,' Rissa replied thoughtfully. 'Marsh's a public man. Even when he makes a fool of himself he does it in public. He's usually an open book. You can see through him in no time. Correct?

'Of course.'

'Except this time he's very furtive. He's not giving anything away. So he has a secret.'

Memories came back to me. There was something strange that time when I saw men with guns in the vicinity of Melbury Hall. We were in the woods beyond the grounds of the Hall. We were not trespassing, but two men with rifles approached us. They kept their distance. They didn't speak. But they watched us intently. Their manner was quietly threatening. We were being warned.

We walked away, back into the village of Combe Melbury. It looked so quiet and peaceful, an idyllic English village where nothing happened. Beyond the windows computer screens flickered as people worked in their home offices. Where once they would have commuted to far away cities, now they sat at home, communicating with the world, and earning the money that paid for their lives in this English idyll.

There was a poster clinging to a board. It was a faded and torn election poster for a candidate who won, but for a party that lost. There was a reforming government which spoke once again of the Socialism everyone thought had been eradicated by limitless prosperity. When the poverty returned the English idyll no longer seemed safe. Some withdrew into villages like this, where the rest of the world was distant. Some became fearful that change would shatter their dreams. There was a nervous edge in the air, even out here in the depths of the tranquil countryside. The nervous edge was at times visible, especially when one saw those men with their guns.

'It can't be, can it?' I said once we were back in our car.

'It could be,' Rissa replied. 'We'll have to find out. It's something we must do. Of course we must.'

It was unthinkable not to agree. I often found myself agreeing with Rissa (sometimes it was diplomatic to do so). But this was different. It was, as she said, serious. I could never wholly condemn Dave Marsh in the past. As must be evident, there was something likeable about him even when he was foolish, or perhaps especially when he was foolish. Now, however, I was not so ready to tolerate and forgive. How could I look away when something wrong, very wrong, was in prospect? That its true nature remained in the shadows didn't lessen the dread. The mystery made it worse.

It was dreadful indeed to think that this really was happening. It was not a game we were playing. We weren't children pretending to be spies. We were mature in attitude and intelligent in our minds and balanced in our judgements, and we had considered the matter carefully. Dave Marsh had become dangerous.

'We need to find out what he's up to,' Rissa said. As ever she was prepared to speak aloud what I dared not think even to myself. We knew, in broad terms, what Marsh was up to. All we needed was confirmation.

Thinking back to those days on the cliff above Paradise Park, it seemed such an innocent time then. It wasn't nearly as innocent as I thought. But, naively or perhaps wisely, I thought it to be innocent at the time. Where others were suspicious or calculating, I believed that benevolence had the advantage. Although experience had not put an end to that belief, I was less sure now of others. What was happening was serious.

'We need to find out,' I agreed.

Three

'There is a question each of us must answer, a question in our work, in our homes, and in the silence of the night. That question is simple. You must ask yourself, do you make mistakes, or do mistakes make you? If the answer to the first part is no, then you're not telling the truth to yourself, and, boy, are you making some mistake. If the answer to the second part is yes, then you need to turn your life around.' Simpson leaned forward to take a sip of water from the coffee table. It was hot under the studio lights. There was this pause, clearly pre-arranged because the host did not interrupt, before Simpson continued his answer: 'My technique can change your life around. And, unless you're perfect, you need to change. We all need to change.'

'And, tell me, how does that relate to your work on *Sunrise Heights*?' the host asked of the spiritual advisor to the daytime soap that attracted both loyalty and derision in perhaps equal measure.

'You mean, why get mixed up in this? Well, I believe that the message can be conveyed in many forms, whether it's Ludwig van Beethoven or rock music. The themes that concerned Shakespeare were love and war and our responsibilities. That's also true of *Sunrise Heights*. Remember Shakespeare was thought not-quite-the-intellectual thing in his day. Well, he is now. So who knows? And, in any case, *Sunrise* is great fun, and I love it.'

Whoops and cheers and prolonged applause followed this. Simpson knew how to work an audience.

'Well,' the host said eventually, 'we'll hear something more about the Simpson Technique after this announcement...'

This was what had become of Simpson. He looked well, although older than in the time I knew him. He looked older than his years. This I put down to experience. Life had given him a harder edge. I saw steel in those eyes. He smiled on his lips, but not in his eyes.

That much was not too surprising. What did surprise was Simpson's successful transformation into an Anglo-American cable television celebrity. I had thought there was more to him. He looked like someone clinging desperately to the edge of the precipice. Beneath the cool exterior was an ice-cold determination, but it was the determination of a man who was surviving against the odds, rather than a man who knew that was easily winning.

'The Simpson Technique is a simple routine you can follow in your own time and in your own way. If you devote just a few minutes of every day to this technique you can improve, you can survive, AND *you can win.*' [Applause.]

'And the technique is?'

'First of all you must remember that each of us should dedicate every day to ourselves. That's so important. You must say, "This is my day." Say that every day. It's your day, not somebody else's. No matter how much people demand this and that of you, and the pressure piles up, and the bills have to be paid, and the dog's sick, and your favourite flower has lost its golden petals – none of that matters because you can rise above everything and let it sort itself out. Don't worry: this is your day.'

There was a ripple of applause before the host interjected: 'But one thing I don't get, Dr. Simpson, is how if it's my day can it be your day too?'

'Because I'm me and you're you. My day isn't your day.'

There was more applause, louder this time, with all the customary whoops and cheers. The banalities bolstered fragile lives. People who were not living their dream found inspiration in Simpson's reassurances. Follow his technique and you can live on Sunrise Heights. It may be that you can stay only thirty minutes every morning, but you can find your place there. You can find your self, your real self, on that imagined hill in that imagined town. It's real to you and to countless others.

We were watching a recording Nerys had sent over. Neither *Sunrise Heights* nor *The Show Business Show* were available to us, as far as we knew. It could have been that some obscure channel carried them, but not within our range of vision. That was no serious loss, but for the chance to see Simpson (and where was that doctorate from?) as he was in his maturity.

'You know who he reminds me of?' Rissa said. 'Don't laugh, but he reminds of Dave Marsh. Yes, I thought you'd laugh.'

'I don't see it.'

'Of course I don't mean there's any physical resemblance,' Rissa explained, patiently rising above my (anticipated) derision. 'But it's the desperate sense of purpose. They share that, you agree?'

'Agreed. Yes.'

'Surviving against the odds - they have that in common. There's the same look each has in his eyes. You noticed it?'

I noticed it. And I agreed that it was unsettling. In their different ways Simpson and Marsh were men with a determination. Quite what each was determined on it was not easy to say. In one sense it made little difference what trajectories they each envisaged for themselves. Each man defined by his sense of determination, they were both unsettling.

Marsh we thought the more unsettling because he was close at hand. Simpson we could see was aiming for cult status. He wanted not just an audience, but devotees. He was sure to find them.

The next guest on the show was a devoted fan, she said, of both Simpson's philosophy of life and *Sunrise Heights*. 'I can't tell you how much I love it,' said the dress designer. 'I find it so inspiring.'

'Do you watch it every day, Suzanne?' the host asked.

'I try to. When I'm working, I really like to watch it then because it, like, gives me ideas.'

'Have you designed for the show?' the host asked.

'We'd love to have you,' Simpson interjected.

'Oh, no,' Suzanne replied. 'You're very kind. You're kind. But, like, *Sunrise* means so much to me, so much. I just couldn't. I need distance. When you're creating something you have to, like, step back. Well, I simply could not do that with something I just adore.'

'Why is that, Suzanne?'

'Oh, it's the clothes, of course. And the houses. Those perfect lives that really aren't so perfect. But they pull through. Everyone pulls through. They, like, win in the end. All those little victories mean so much in life, don't they?'

'That's so profound,' Simpson agreed.

'Why, thank you, Doctor.' There was delighted applause at that.

'Tell me, Suzanne,' the host of the show asked, 'who is your favourite character in *Sunrise Heights*?'

'Oh, let me see, that has got to be Brandy.' One or two gasps of approval were audible as she spoke the name of this character. 'I just love Brandy O'Connell. She is just so, like, real. I mean, Brandy is not the perfect woman. So she's really true to life. She gets things wrong. She makes bad moves. She can be pretty dumb sometimes. Well, I think, heck, that's just like me and everybody I have ever known.'

'But she's pretty.'

'She is so pretty. She, like, knows how to bring out her beauty. She is always smart. And, I mean, she's often pretty smart in her brain, too. That's what I appreciate about her. She's such an inspiration. Brandy shows how a woman can be attractive and gracious and good without, like, surrendering herself to men's idea of what a woman should be. Brandy is *her* idea of what *she* should be. That's so, like, truly inspiring. So, thank you, Dr. Simpson. Thank you.' Thunderous applause. A crescendo of cheers.

I thought back to that night in the garden. Before he fell Simpson had said that very curious remark, 'If I close my eyes I'm invisible.' I think it may have been the last thing he said before he vanished into the darkness. He was on the borderline of madness that evening so that I didn't take too seriously what he said. But when I thought of that remark it seemed hauntingly strange. Did Simpson really believe he could control reality?

As for Marsh, he was seeking something we could not so easily locate. He lacked subtlety and finesse. His goal would be more naïve or more crude. Looking back, I see how everything pointed in only one direction. If I ignored the indicators it was because I thought better of people. For all his faults, I continued to think of Dave Marsh, the amiable buffoon. I couldn't accept anything darker. Why should I?

The truth remained in the shadows. One or two curious things happened, however. I thought more than once I saw Gelina, although I knew she was far away. So convinced was I that it was she that I called Nerys who assured me Gelina was in Hollywood. She had seen her only recently. She didn't say how recently. I knew how time passed so quickly. A person can travel very far in a few hours. I was almost convinced it was Gelina I glimpsed from time to time. Had Dave Marsh forgiven her? And, if so, why? What was happening?

Of this I said nothing to Rissa, fearing she would accuse me of indulging in conspiracy theories. We had to keep closely to facts of which we were certain. I could not be certain it was anything other than a phantom of coincidence. Gelina was a type. There were many like her. That is, there were many who aspired to be like her.

Then there were those who aspired to nothing. They were the ones who might easily be led who knew where. Trish was too extreme to be typical of anything. But one thing she said I remembered: 'I wonder what it's like to be the government. I mean, do they have people to tell you what to do when you meet the Queen? And if you're government you can do what you like. You can have people killed, say, and no fucker can stop you. You can bomb America or China if you want. That's what I'd do. Might as well.'

What struck me about that speech was her indifference to the reality of what she was saying. She talked of war as if it were a football game. In that respect she was no different in kind from the people who bought clothes made in Asian sweatshops, knowing that the workers were paid a pittance. She was no different in kind from the people who did not count the enemy's dead in a war. Trish was extreme because she was profoundly disturbed. Everything about her was exaggerated and distorted. But her attitude was different only in kind. Her values were commonplace.

As for Gelina, she differed from many only in the

degree of her achievement. She not only had sensitive talent to create, she had the ice-hard talent to pursue that creativity. She was intelligent. How thoughtful she was, how deeply she felt, were questions I could not answer. All the time I was watching Gelina so carefully. I had the advantage that she didn't know that I was looking. I saw her as I had not been able to see before. I saw a number of things. I saw especially that Gelina was a type who would make a very deadly enemy.

Four

It was a fleshy hand that shook mine. I had not forgotten the texture of that hand. The warmth was familiar, too. Dave Marsh clearly thought of me as an old friend whom he was so genuinely pleased to see again. I had anticipated a coolness in manner, an air of suspicion, but there seemed none. We had not parted well at the last meeting, but that now was forgotten. In some ways Marsh hadn't changed despite everything. That, of course, was what we needed.

For this to work Marsh had to feel at ease with us. He had yet to meet Rissa. Inevitably he was charmed. Most of his attention was directed to her. That was how we had planned it. I had to take a backseat role. It was Rissa who did the talking, Rissa who asked the questions.

It was quite a performance. She knew perfectly how to judge her responses, how to behave, how to look, how to disarm Marsh so that he might reveal more than he intended of what we needed to know.

I could barely believe it was Rissa as she breathlessly asked her wide-eyed questions, and giggled in response when he spoke. She was elegantly dressed for the occasion. Fluttering her long lashes, and pouting her smile, Rissa let her silken legs stretch as, hands on hips, she leaned toward our host so that he might see her necklace sparkle, and breathe in the fragrance of her Chanel, and catch the light rustle of her satin dress.

'Anyway,' Marsh said, his attention fixed on Rissa, 'it's good to see you both, and to meet you at last, young lady.'

'I'm so pleased to meet, you, Mr Marsh. I've heard so much about you.'

'Nothing bad I hope?' Marsh predictably ventured. Rissa only giggled.

Marsh was wondering, because men at such times do wonder, what was happening beneath the dress. Imagining what privately she was wearing, Marsh's mind was wandering through clouds of crimson lace and satin. A wave of envy toward me darkened Marsh's countenance for a second. In another second he covered himself well by offering more wine. Then he turned back to Rissa who remained attentive to Marsh as if there were no other man in the room.

I was almost jealous. I had seen such a performance before, but not from Rissa. Where impressionable Gelina in her ambition had been open to suggestion, Rissa, I knew, despised Marsh. For his part, Marsh he was too enamoured of her superficial charms to think that such a sweet girl could be a perceptive woman. The truth, as I well knew, was that Rissa would have seen through him at once had she known nothing about him before this first meeting. She read people well, and Marsh, of course was so easy to read.

'You've got something there, young man,' Marsh said when Rissa excused herself for a moment. 'Smashing. You lucky little sod. Still, you're young, the pair of you, and good luck to you. I'm doing fine as I am.'

Inevitably the subject of holidays was raised. 'Go abroad much?' Marsh asked. 'I used to, but I'm never sure about foreigners. It's the language. You hear them and you wonder what they're saying. Beats me how they understand one another. To be honest, I don't think they do half the time. A lot of it's guesswork. No wonder there's so much trouble in the world. Of course we have the advantage, with the Bible being written in English. It gives us the advantage, I always think.'

'It's good to see you, Dave. I really wanted to see you.' I was not lying, but I wasn't being wholly honest either. I wanted to see Marsh for a very different reason than the one I gave. 'I see now I let you down, Dave.'

'Me? No. Forget it. Forget it, old pal.' Marsh wanted to think only about Rissa. 'So you'll be getting married, the two of you, I expect? You don't want to let her slip through your fingers.' He paused before whispering in a confidential tone, 'Talking of fingers - a woman I know, you should see what her fingers can do.' Marsh laughed before going through the necessary pretence of being slightly shocked at his artless candour.

'Anyone I might know?' I asked.

'Now, careful,' he admonished me, exchanging another laugh. He poured more wine.

I was careful not to drink too much, whereas Marsh was as unwise as ever. In that, too, he had not changed.

He had not changed except, perhaps, for the worse. He seemed to be drinking even more rashly than before, or so it seemed. It may have seemed that way simply because I'd forgotten how heavily Marsh drank. And yet I felt sure that his problem had increased to dangerous levels. He was drinking when we arrived. I suspected that he had been drinking all day. I suspected it would be the same every day.

The effect on his body and mind could be surmised by the florid complexion and the slurring of speech. Marsh didn't notice Rissa at the top of the staircase. She lingered, then moved out of sight so that she could listen unobserved.

'Women,' Marsh began, 'I wonder about them.' He paused. 'I mean, the ones you want, they let you down. The others'll do anything. Doesn't make much sense to me. Does it to you? No, of course it bloody doesn't. Doesn't make sense to any man. So that's when you ask yourself why? Why?'

'Why what, Dave?'

'Why do they make you pay? Women, they make sure you pay.'

'I'm not sure what you mean, Dave,' I said, truthfully.

'Look, find me a woman who just gives you what you want.'

There was another pause. This time it was not because Marsh could not think what to say next. It was a calculated moment, allowing me the opportunity to speak. I knew that Marsh wanted me to say something. I could feel his mind willing me to speak. If I spoke as he wished me to speak, then I would be his true friend. I would gain his confidence. And so I spoke. I said, 'But,

Dave, do you know of such a woman?'

'I might do,' he replied quietly and seriously.

'A man sometimes needs...' I began.

'I know what a man needs, old friend. I know.'

Rissa made a noise upstairs, opening and closing a door to indicate that she was coming down. She and I did dare exchange a look. What I saw was giggly little Rissie falter on the stairs, as if she had drunk rather too much.

'Perhaps if we have coffee in the drawing room?' Marsh suggested, ushering both of us in. Rissa got most of his attention. She made a fuss about sitting, smoothing her dress several times before she sat in the comfortable armchairs of the drawing room. Then she wriggled and giggled again. Her performance amused me, for it was so convincing. Marsh was completely taken in. He was captivated. She was what he expected a woman to be.

It was a measure of his corruption that Marsh saw nothing untoward in my question about a certain sort of woman. He didn't ask why I should desire anything more than this lovely creature. He thought it natural. I thought it perverse.

The coffee was accompanied by liqueurs. I accepted chartreuse. Rissa thought it better not to, accepting only on Marsh's insistence. That, too, was integral to her performance.

'You see,' Marsh began as if in reply to a point another had made, 'I feel that two young people like you, well, you're the cream of our nation. No, I mean that. I mean, I look at some people, then I look at you. And I think that this is the future worth fighting for. I mean, you're not like some I could mention. I had my doubts at one time about this young man here. Oh yes, I had my doubts, but I see I didn't need to doubt for one minute you'd turn out well.' He held out his arm in an admiring gesture. Then he turned to Rissa. 'And you, my lovely, are just perfect. I don't mind saying I wish I was a few years younger. But, be that as it may, you're a lucky couple. If there more like you two then we'd have nothing to fear.'

'That's very kind of you, Dave,' I said.

'You see, he's so polite!' Marsh exclaimed in delight. 'I don't know what is with you people. I just don't know how you do it. It's the schools they send you to, I'm sure of it. And at home, too, wasn't it? There was music, books, theatre in your childhood. That was an education. You were brought up to appreciate a refined view of life. I'm not saying your family are rich. There's culture there, though. That's what makes the difference. That I'm sure of.'

I remembered Rissa's litany of how we should be this evening: conformist in taste and conventional in manner; immaculate in presentation, impeccable in style; polished and polite and utterly unthreatening. We performed a parody of a conservative society's wishes against which we had rebelled by being individuals and not types. Marsh wanted the stereotypes. He wanted to feel safe.

'The problem is,' Marsh continued, 'we have plenty

to fear. You've only to look about you. I've said for years that our values are threatened. It's our own fault if we let things slide further.' He leaned forward, lowering his voice. 'At times I feel a stranger in my own country. There are places where you'll hardly see a white face. Where are all the British, I ask. Driven out of their communities by riots and robberies and a general disregard for civilization which has made us all live by the law of the jungle.'

'I'd hate to live in the jungle,' Rissa said. 'I'd not feel safe.' Her hands held her hips protectively again. She looked appealingly vulnerable, the pampered white girl facing the savage hordes. 'I'd not feel safe at all.'

'You're not safe now. None of us are with so many savages parading about the streets. They've no self-control. If they see something they grab it. They don't work for it. And that's the society we've become.'

'How awful,' Rissa said, as if she were hearing some appalling news for the first time.

'Something must be done,' I said with a gravity more appropriate to an original comment of some substance. I was enjoying my part in this performance now.

'I blame the intellectuals. We've let the so-called experts run riot with their statistics and their theories, when everyone decent Englishman knows that it's bloody nonsense. It makes me sick to the gills to think that this is happening, and we can see it happening, and we do nothing. Well, all I can say is it is time something was done. You're right there, young man.'

Both Rissa and I hoped that Marsh was going to say

more. He did look for a second or two as if he might say more. He was weighing up in his mind how far he could go, how much he could say. We both separately were willing to say more.

I wondered whether I should say something to encourage him. Rissa, however, stepped in. Hers was much the better enticement. 'It's Socialism, isn't it, Mr Marsh?' I noted that this time he liked the deference. There was no 'Call me Dave.' In that respect he had changed. He was someone who had sought for himself an air of authority. He was someone who had tasted power, or at least had glimpsed power. That had to mean that Marsh's ambitions went beyond the city council. Quite where the ambition was leading we needed to find out. 'Daddy says Socialism nearly destroyed us.'

'Well, my dear, your father's absolutely right. Socialism did nearly destroy us. But it's a menace that hasn't gone away. And I don't just mean this left-wing government. I mean Socialism by stealth. I mean the enemy within the walls: subversive ideas being taught in our schools, and piped day and night into our homes. Not to mention all the undesirables crowding our cities and roaming our countryside. Well, I for one have just about enough of it.'

'You should stand for Parliament, Dave,' I suggested.

'This is beyond Parliament. You can't play by the rules when you're dealing with menace on the scale I'm talking about. Evil has to be rooted out at source. It's the only way. Well, it's a fact. It's a plain and simple fact. A child of seven can see that society must live by rules, and those rules must be obeyed. Believe you me, it's a fact, right enough. As far as I can see Socialism's just another word for bad manners. I mean, business needs a loyal workforce. That much is effin' obvious – pardonay mon fronsay - but loyalty, honesty and hard work are alien words in the left-wing alphabet. You get the overpaid intellectuals moaning about this and that instead of telling people what is right and what is wrong. Well, it sickens me to think of it happening under our very noses.'

'It's very frightening to think of it happening in our country. I mean, this is England,' Rissa said.

'And it always will be. Don't you worry. Some of us are prepared to stand up and be counted.'

'Include me in, Dave,' I responded, not too eagerly. I had to judge the correct measure of enthusiasm. I had to gain Marsh's trust. He did not say more, however, except to brush it aside as 'men's talk' before moving on to lighter topics. We had got some way, but not very far.

Leaving at the end of the evening, I half-whispered the suggestion that Marsh and I talk further. Marsh was silent. I expected the silence to continue. Very likely, I surmised, he did not trust quite enough to confide his plans. I doubted that he ever should do so.

When a few days later the call came it was a surprise. Marsh had been tempted by the bait. I had Rissa to thank. Her performance had been superb. It took its toll her, though. In the car she exploded with an alarming howl of rage. She was slightly ashamed at having to go against all her convictions of womanhood. While remaining very feminine, Rissa loathed the frivolous and silly as much as I loathed the correct and conservative. We had explored our alternative selves. For one evening we had played the parts that we might have acted all our lives. We both recognized what was potentially within us. It was troubling to think that from the shadows we could summon those other selves we despised.

Rissa warned me to be careful when I told her about the call. 'I don't know where that bastard is going,' she said with feeling, 'but I don't want you to be hurt.'

Five

In a rural community what news there is everyone hears very quickly. A murder is rare (though you'd hardly think so from those television detective shows). When a body is found everyone hears about it, and everyone feels connected in some way. The victim is someone everyone knows someone who knew her. But not in the case of the unknown young woman find dead by the roadside near Bradcombe.

Nobody came forward to claim her. There was nothing to identify her. It was a body found one Sunday morning by someone driving to church. It was a body from which all breath, all mind, all personality, all spirit had departed. Dressed in once-elegant, now muddied and blooded, party clothes, this slender heap of lifeless waste disturbed all who saw it, and shocked all who heard of it.

Extensive enquiries in the small town of Bradcombe offered no clues. An obvious place to begin forensic enquiries was the Moon and Goose, an ancient inn that had become a hotel with a good restaurant. Entry was strictly regulated. Patrons had to be smart, as the dead young woman had been. It was thought likely she had been at the Moon and Goose. That line of enquiry, however, led nowhere.

The possibility was that the victim had been murdered elsewhere, then dumped some distance away. Such a thing was not unknown. The whisper went about that the woman was very likely from Bristol. This speculation rapidly acquired the status of an established fact. Expensively dressed in exclusive and highly fashionable styles, she was not likely to be local. This was a smart city girl.

The autopsy revealed that she had recently had sex. There were traces of alcohol and cocaine. She had been killed by a bullet in the back of the head, like an execution. There were bruises and cuts to her body, like the victim of torture. This was no lover's quarrel that had got out of hand. This was no crime of frustrated passion. The woman had been murdered deliberately and carefully and professionally. The death itself would have been instantaneous, but the preliminary was likely to have been prolonged, painful and terrifying. No doubt she had died distraught in mind and destroyed in spirit. No-one saw or heard it happen. Or if anyone did, no-one intervened. She was abandoned as if she were nothing.

All enquiries having led nowhere, the speculation now was that the victim had been not the society girl she seemed, but an expensive prostitute. Furthermore, if her death meant nothing to anyone, as seemed to be the case, the likelihood was that she was an illegal immigrant, someone who did not exist and who would not be missed. Trafficked from a remote and poor corner of Eastern Europe, she had been subjected to a life one dare not imagine. Attempting to escape, she was murdered as a warning to others of her kind.

Slaves have no rights. They have nothing except

their servitude, like a prison sentence without hope of remission. All talk of work and money had vanished. The enticing promises soon were seen clearly as cynical lies. And in some basement or high tower of a foreign country a woman, no more than twenty, was visited by men whose language she barely understood, but whose desires were universal in the pain and fear they engendered. She was punished for being pretty. She was punished for being poor.

Into our quiet country landscape came a reminder of the world's evil, the power that the selfish have to destroy all beauty, all hope, all love. 'She couldn't be a local,' everyone said with absolute certainty. 'There's nothing like that round here, is there? Well, I mean, there isn't, is there?'

A wave of apprehension passed over the area, like an enormous shadow. Uncertainty was written on the faces of people at the bus stop. There was a tremor in voices at the supermarket. Anxious parents supervised their children with extra diligence. There were calls for more vigilant and visible police patrols. There were letters and speeches demanding that action be taken. 'We aren't safe any more,' was the general comment, said with feeling.

One evening Rissa and I were stopped on our way to the Moon and Goose. We went there from time to time. There was nothing certain to link it to the murder. Life, we decided, must go on. If we were to remain in the area we had to live our usual life as best we could. Affected as we were by the murder, we thought it important to maintain a sense of customary routine and everyday things. It was the banalities of life that could anchor a community at such a time. For the time being we wanted nothing more unusual to happen.

We drove our usual route, avoiding Glastonbury by taking the road that passed quite close to Combe Melbury. We came this way quite regularly. It was always quiet. Rarely did we see another car. It suited us to go that way.

In the fading light, although we were familiar with the route, we took a wrong turning. I drove down a narrow lane, hoping that it would lead us toward a road we knew. There was a group of uniformed men ahead. They were standing before a barrier, like a customs post.

A figure in uniform came up to our car. He was dressed like a policeman, which is what at first we took him to be. Then we saw that he was a private security guard with no legal authority to demand questions of us.

'We has orders to ask people what business they have here,' the guard said.

'This is a public highway,' I said.

'Actually, sir, this is a private road, the property of Melbury Hall. We got the right to ask you what your business is here.' The guard's words were polite, whereas his tone had an air of menace, and his whole manner was foreboding. He had power. He was well aware that he had power. He enjoyed the status it gave him. It raised his spirits. His eyes were mocking us.

'As far as I'm concerned,' I said, 'I'm not trespassing. There was no indication that this is a private road.'

'It is private, sir. You got no right, sir. You understand, sir?'

'Well, perhaps you can tell me how we get to Bradcombe on a public highway.'

'I'm asking the questions now. I'm here to ask you to produce some identification. You need to say who the fuck you are, sir '

'You know that's none of your business.'

'In fact, you're trespassing on private property. In fact, we got the right to detain you.'

'You have no such right.'

'We has orders.' The guard had abandoned all pretence of courtesy. He was giving orders. He demanded that we obey, while anticipating that we were going to refuse. It was a game he was playing.

'Look, just let us turn round.'

'I can't allow that, not till I've seen your identification. You could be anyone. You could be media reporters. You could be terrorists. You could be anything. I mean, why would innocent people be trespassing on private property? Obvious you got something to hide if you don't let us know who you are and what business you got driving here on private property.'

'This is absurd. You have no right.'

'You got no right, not on this land. Not here. You know where this is? Course you do. Why else would you be snooping around. That's why we're here – to protect this private property from unwanted trespassers who got no right.'

'I think you've made your point,' I said. 'This is not a public highway. We took a wrong turning. There was no indica...'

'I don't want to hear no more.' The guard was speaking to me while his attention was fixed on Rissa. He regarded Rissa for a long time. She looked away, but he continued to note all he saw of her with brazen contempt for her humanity in his libidinous gaze. Finally he said, 'You could really earn some money, darlin'.' Then he looked at me, willing me to challenge him.

'Bastard,' Rissa hissed in contempt. The guard's face took on an ugly smile. It was the smile of someone capable of doing anything without giving it a moment's thought. All that mattered was the sensation. Indifferent to others, his cold eyes watched for the chance of a momentary thrill. The bruises and the blood meant nothing to him. The screaming he would surely enjoy.

'Look,' I told the guard, 'we're going now.' I turned the engine on as Rissa reached for her phone. 'So if you wouldn't mind...'

Then came the moment we could barely believe. What happened was one of those acts that seem impossible yet are undeniably real. We had been driving peaceably through the Somerset countryside. Now we were confronted with a reality that confirmed our worst suspicions. What couldn't be true evidently was. It was undeniable, however unlikely it seems now to write this. We were confronted with an appalling reality in sober truth.

To our astonishment the guard produced a gun. He pointed the gun at us. 'I mind. I mind very much. I got authority,' he said. 'I got authority. This. And what you got? You got FUCKING NOTHING!' He screamed those last words from a vicious, ugly mouth, a seriously, dangerously violent mouth. He was living out trite sensations of power as if it were a movie that had come alive.

There was no arguing with him. He was out of control, and he had a gun. What was it Dave Marsh had said? 'You can't play by the rules.' He was not playing by the rules. These men under his command were acting outside of society. They were acting according to Marsh's vision of the world.

What we had glimpsed of that vision was a strange fantasy realized. Idle talk had been translated into action. This was the mindset of a vision out of control. The gun directed at us was loaded. The guard had been prepared to fire. Provoked, he would have fired the gun. I doubted if that was the first time he had fired a gun at someone.

Other guards were hurrying to our car. Fortunately for us, one of the men carefully ushered away the guard with the gun. Another guard ordered us to leave our car.

It was a familiar voice. His face, too, was vaguely familiar, but I couldn't think from where. Then Mick said, 'Fuck me. I know you, don't I?'

Four:

Coming Down as Rain

Geoffrey Heptonstall

One

'I know you, don't I?'

There was an old man sitting under the trees in the park. It was a cold day, the coldest of the season so far. There was no wind. The air was still in the frost. Leaves lay on the ground, dry and crisp. They crunched underfoot. On such a day they were going to be swept away. A park attendant was sorting out his machine in a distant corner where a padlocked pavilion housed the equipment he needed to keep the park in order.

The old man was dressed only in a short jacket. Hatless and gloveless, he looked very cold. He looked dangerously cold for a man of his years. He looked frail in body. I suspected he was a little mad. The old grow mad in varying degrees. He was perhaps in the uncertain middle ground between eccentricity and dementia. What were chances, I wondered, if he did not look after himself? He needed a warm, winter coat. More than that, he needed to be indoors. Surely he had somewhere to go? Even the old, even the mad have somewhere to go.

I walked down Guinea Lane, diverting into the park to reflect on all that had happened. So much had happened in a brief time. The ordeal was fading from memory now. It no longer upset me. We had a new life far away, a gallery by the sea. There we were going to raise our children, children who were to know nothing of what had happened, nothing of the effect it had wrought on us.

Worse than the trial itself were the dreams that came later. As with a death of someone close, at the time you feel strong, able to cope. It was later that the awfulness of it all came upon me. I felt overwhelmed and oppressed by the things I had been witness to over the years. Of course I had been at a distance, but I was never too far away. There had been hints for a long time. I knew something was wrong. I had known for a long time. My hope with Caroline was to escape, and to live a good life. My hope with Rissa was to live a good life. But, once entangled, I found I had no means of breaking free.

Above everything I wished to be innocent again. But in the garden – in the summerhouse – began a train of events leading inevitably as they did to those dark, deadly affairs. I was only a witness. No more than an onlooker, I felt the effects of the corruption that would not let me be. I always was felt drawn back, not by my own prurient will, but by chance, by fate that intruded into my life, into our life, when we wanted to live at peace with the world.

A witness at the trial, I felt punished as if I were among the accused. I wanted to run out of the court and never to return, and never to learn what happened. I wanted to pretend none of it had happened. I had often felt like that about bad things. It was silly, but it was to me feeling that came very naturally.

Simpson on that talk show we saw said, 'There is a question each of us must answer, a question in our work, in our homes, and in the silence of the night. That question is simple. You must ask yourself do you make mistakes, or do mistakes make you? If the answer to the first part is no, then you're not telling the truth to yourself, and, boy, are you making some mistake. If the answer to the second part is yes, then you need to turn your life around.' At the time I thought it typically slick of him. So it was.

That much was obvious to me. I had understood about Simpson back in the garden soon after we first met. I understood that Simpson was clever. Especially as he matured, he did speak a certain amount of sense. It is true that we can be defined by our limitations if we allow them. We ought to be defined by our possibilities, but that takes qualities – confidence, courage, tenacity – that are not easily acquired. They're not easily recognized. Each of us could be more than we are.

They, like me, had been called to give evidence. Where I had very little to say, their testimonies were the ones that were likely to secure a conviction. They knew much more than I did about the curious events to which I was only a distant onlooker seeing in the night mist something I could not makes sense of.

The police took a statement from me, and one from Rissa. There was little either of us could say. It was a surprise when we were summoned as witnesses. All we were able to say was that it was too dark for me to be sure.

A trial is not the glamorous event we see portrayed in the movies. There was a coldness about it, a sense of harsh reality, an indifferent matter-of-fact feeling about the proceedings. Counsel for the defence could have been counsel for prosecution with as much conviction and determination. It was not a game, but it was played like a game without a game's passion and energy. At times serious matters affecting many lives were spoken of as abstractions.

When a witness faltered, when a voice quivered, or a body trembled, or a tear came into a witness's eye the men and women of law were unmoved. What they wanted was the version of the truth that suited their purpose. They didn't care what happened to anyone subsequently when the truth was exposed.

I did care. Rissa cared. Everyone cared because our lives had been tarnished. A layer of innocence had been stripped bare. It affected me deeply. For a while I wondered if I was going to trust anyone ever again. I wondered if I knew anyone. 'I know you, don't I?' I wanted to say to everyone. I looked at myself, and asked that question of myself. It took time before I could answer.

One day I simply said yes. And I smiled. For the first time in what seemed like years, but was only weeks, I smiled. Rissa and I drove down until we reached the edge of land. And there we decided we were going to live. Yes, I said. Yes.

Two

'This is not the way I wanted it. None of it has been the way I expected things to go. To be honest with you I sometimes wonder if I'm not dreaming. It's all a big mistake. Everything's been twisted to make me look something I'm not. It's a disgrace, I tell you.'

Dave Marsh sat at the table in the visiting room of the prison where he awaited trial. I was not to be called as a witness, of course they didn't need me. I knew almost nothing. I had been questioned. That was all. I had so little to tell.

Dave Marsh had a great deal to tell. He wanted a listener. He chose me. It may have been that I was one on a list of possible contacts. I wondered if others had been approached, only to refuse. Letters went unanswered as Marsh, an increasingly desperate figure, sought out someone he had known and continued to hope he could trust. He wrote to me.

'Ignore it,' Rissa had said. At first I agreed. Never a real friend, Marsh now was at best an object of pity in my eyes. I could feel no sympathy. Everything had been forfeited when the truth began to emerge. That he was guilty we had no doubt.

Of course Marsh didn't see it like that: 'What I'm trying to say is that everything went wrong, and don't know how. It beats me fair and square. I got the shock of my life when they arrested me. I didn't know what was going on. Headlights, barking dogs, armed police bursting into the room. I didn't know what was going on. Of course I can see how it looked: I was changing while the girls were taking a shower. But it was not, in fact, the sordid incident it seemed. Far from it. I was auditioning the girls for an entertainment spot at the Hall. That was a perfectly innocent fact, but, of course, the press saw it different. It made me look like I don't know what. Very bad timing. And it's just typical of this whole affair. Well, I dare say it'll be sorted out soon. I've got a crack team of lawyers onto it. Fortunately, I have every faith in British justice.'

The feeling was not reciprocated. Arrested, Marsh had been indicted for serious crimes of which conspiracy to murder was only one. So much had been reported even before the trial that Marsh was one of the most notorious figures in the land.

It was not comfortable to think that Rissa and I were involved in all this at the margin. That we were regarded as innocent bystanders accused of nothing was no relief. We felt tainted by the proximity to these crimes. This was especially true for me. There was no doubting the high seriousness of these matters. All of Marsh's protestations could not lighten the oppressive air of corruption pervading everything to do with Dave Marsh.

I had tried to distance myself. For a long time I neither saw nor heard anything of him. When he asked me to call I could have refused. A blend of courtesy and curiosity overcame my objections, and I went to see him. But that was all. I made it plain I wanted nothing to do with Melbury Hall. Then curiosity got the better of me. We tried to reconnoitre the Hall. Then we found ourselves facing one of the militia's guns.

A cache of weapons, explosives and uniforms was found at the Hall. We were astonished. Such things belonged in the realm of sensational fiction. It didn't seem credible in the world we knew. That was the whole point of the militia; it had a sense of fantasy about it. I thought of Marsh drinking at the club bar with friends, and starting a sentence that began 'You know what this country needs is...' It is a sentence that ends with an image of order that no-one takes seriously.

However much his hearers would like to see a society ordered and obedient, the nearest they could find was the solace of submissive Far Eastern and Slavonic young women, costumed and painted, serving drinks and fine dining and whatever else a man of money can buy. 'When we had empire,' such men said, 'women like that were everywhere. And everyone knew their place.'

Melbury Hall was Dave Marsh's empire. It, however, was not enough. He had tasted the power of what he could do, and that taste had never left him. Protestations of innocence were so obviously self-deception.

'It's a lie about me trying to kill Simpson,' Marsh told me in the prison visiting room. 'It was an accident. I mean, you're as much to blame as I am. You were there.'

'I didn't see you,' I told him firmly.

'No, well, I kept quiet, listening. I was listening to the two of you. I didn't understand what it was between you. Something about an ear ring. Anyway, I was there listening. That was all. I did not push him over the cliff. That was not my intention at all.'

I couldn't think of Marsh now as I had before. Any indulgence of his obtuse bigotry had been forfeited. I was looking at a man I knew to be guilty. The trial had yet to be held. He was innocent in the eyes of law until all the evidence was presented, and a jury had decided. The verdict on at least some of the charges was foregone. I was looking at a man whom everyone knew to be guilty. I listened, not knowing what questions to ask of this stupid, dangerous man whose friendship, never too strong, I had long since forsaken.

'I wanted to speak to Simpson. Gelina was thinking of going back to him. I was angry with him. But it was an accident. He wouldn't stop laughing. I couldn't stand that laughter. But, I swear I never meant anything to happen.'

No, it wasn't intentional. Marsh hadn't planned anything in particular. A moment's thought would have told him confrontation was going to end badly. Marsh didn't think ahead. He simply went into the garden.

All those years I had felt some responsibility. Caroline had blamed me, of course. Even Rissa's assurances couldn't remove every trace of self-doubt. And it turned it was nothing to do with me. I heard laughter in the dark of a moonless, clouded night. I saw nothing. I didn't know even that Marsh was there, creeping about silently, waiting for an opportunity to hit back in his jealousy.

'I defy anyone to prove that I am a murderer. It's simply not true. There's no proof. It's all gossip. You know what gossip is like. It gets the wrong end of the stick. Well, that's what's happened. But the truth will out, believe you me.'

'And what is the truth, Dave?'

'I had nothing to do with that Russian girl. I don't think I ever met her. She might have worked at the Hall, but we had so many passing through. An agency sent them. I didn't know who half of them were.'

Marsh paused. He took in an enormous breath. He was sweating profusely. He blamed it on the heat. 'You can't imagine what I've been through,' he said. 'They make you feel worthless. That's the worst of it. To be treated like some criminal. And I've never lifted a finger against anyone. I defy anyone to come forward and bring proof that I have acted out of the law.'

The self-pitying pleas were becoming predictable and tedious. Marsh had nothing to say of any substance. He simply wanted to declare his innocence as if that declaration would cleanse him of all responsibility.

'This is not the way I wanted it,' Marsh said once more. 'Events got out of hand. I didn't know what they were doing. How was I to know? You tell me: how was I to know? The point is that any reasonable human being looking at the facts of the situation is going to come to the conclusion that justice has not been done. Not that I feel bitter about it. I just want to restore a little sanity to the situation which has got well out of control. If I am in any way to blame it is that I was too trusting of people. Well, it could happen to anyone. The more you trust people, the more they let you down. And I have been let down right, left and centre.'

There was another pause as Marsh's eyes looked into mine. There was a look at once imploring and defiant. He was never going to admit any responsibility for anything that happened.

'I mean, why should I want to kill someone I valued as a friend? He was more than a friend to me. That young man was one of the most intelligent and interesting human beings it has ever been my privilege to meet. Yes, I was momentarily annoyed with him. But that does not mean I held him in less than total respect. I wouldn't harm a hair on his body. I just can't think why he'd say otherwise. It seems I was wrong about him. Well, that's me all over, isn't it? Too bloody trusting. And look where it's got me.'

The walls of the visiting room were painted a dull cream. All the woodwork was green. The warders stood watchfully at a distance. They looked like men accustomed to violence. I was reminded of the militia. I could not forget that the militia was under the ultimate command of the prisoner the other side of the table. Surely he must have seen it was going to end like this?

'It looks as though I was wrong about Evangelina, too. I was certainly wrong about her. I loved her, you know. I loved everything about her – her face, her hair, her clothes, not to mention the way she talked and walked. She was such a lovely girl. Who couldn't love a girl like her, eh? That Rissa of yours, now you're a lucky man there, mate, I'll tell you. It's the way they giggle I like.'

For the first time Marsh's face relaxed, but it was not for long. 'Not that you can ever trust a woman,' he said icily. 'They're not like men. No man would do what she did. No would ever do what that bitch did. I saw those photographs. Evidence, the police said. Lies more like. You know, she'd been stalking me. A perfectly innocent situation is made to look like something out of... like something out of a sick mind. And that's what that bloody bitch has got – a sick mind. No decent woman would think of doing what she did. To think I ever loved her. And she said she loved me. Well, not in so many words, but she did marry me, after all.'

It was getting dark. The sun already was setting at this late time of year. It was going to be dark soon. I had quite a long drive back.

'Well, I happen to believe that marriage means something,' Marsh continued. 'She was no better than a...' He looked down for a second. 'I didn't know about what was going on. I didn't know about those girls. I thought it was all above board. I told you about my plans for the Hall. I said it was going to be in the best taste. And as far as I'm concerned it was. If money changed hands it was none of my business. I'm not responsible for what other people do, am I? How can I be? Answer me that. I can't be, can I?'

There was nothing I could say. There was nothing I wanted to say. I couldn't speak in the way Marsh clearly wished. I could not agree. I owed him no favours.

Even had I assured him he was blameless my words were not capable of doing what he desperately wish were true. Nothing I said was capable of establishing his innocence, of absolving him, of opening the prison gates so that Dave Marsh might become the respected citizen again. There was no going back. And he must have known that.

'Nobody was held against their will. It's a lie to say otherwise. That's what they're saying, you know. I'm charged with abduction and false imprisonment. Would you credit it? Would you credit the lengths to which Socialists will go to destroy someone whose only crime is to believe in his country and to stand up for it.'

'Dave,' I said, 'there's the militia. I saw them, remember?'

'Militia? Don't give me militia. They were security guards. I employed men I could trust to defend my property. Let me tell you straight away that a man has a right to defend his property as surely as he has a right to defend his country. It's the right of every freeborn Englishman to protect and defend what is rightfully his by law established. You don't need to tell me what is mine.'

'But the photographs?'

'What of them. It was a joke when I dressed up in that uniform. It was a bit of fun. And those guns, they weren't real. As far as I was concerned it was a bit of fun. That's all it was meant to be, all of it. If it got a bit out of hand, well, I'm sorry about that. As I say, it was all meant as a joke. Some people can't take a joke.

Madam certainly can't, not with her bloody camera giving totally the wrong impression. Who says the camera can't lie?'

'And the women at the Hall?'

'Photographs taken through windows – you don't believe they tell the whole story? Things could get me bit boisterous, I'll grant you. Red-blooded men like sexy girls. Nothing wrong with that, for fuck's bloody sake. I'm sick of all this hypocrisy. Every normal man likes a bit of excitement. It's only natural, and it's not against the law – yet.'

And so he went on... My attention wandered. I began to think of the cedars of Lebanon in Wells, then of the copper beeches in Paradise Park, of the lime trees in the garden where Caroline and I lived. I thought about her, and how she had faded. I thought of Rissa, walking with me toward by the river.

I had forgotten the old man in the park by the time I saw Rissa waiting in the cafe. He came back to me only as I began to write of that day when I walked for one final glimpse of the past. If Dave Marsh were ever to be released he should have been that old man in the park.

It wasn't Marsh of course. Marsh's sentence was a life sentence. That was, we thought, very likely to be a death sentence, for it was doubtful if he could have survived prison. Released, he was sure to have been very old. But I don't imagine he made it that far. I see him as broken in a crowded cell of a stinking prison. I see him declining rapidly in spirit, then mind, then body.

We heard nothing of him after the trial. We made no enquiries. As far as we were concerned he disappeared into the life of a convict, with few rights and few comforts, many privations and many humiliations. He was confined with other desperate men considered a danger. Most were violent. Some were mad. None respected him. None respected themselves. Marsh had lost everything in a game of chance he played so recklessly when the odds were against him.

A few others were tried with Marsh. The actual murderer was someone I thought I recognized. Dennis Mackay I did know. He was charged with possession of illegal weapons. A business associate of Marsh's was charged with financial irregularities. But Marsh was the principal culprit.

It was obvious to us that evidence had been suppressed. There must have been some photographs of visitors to Melbury Hall that influential men preferred to forget. Decisions had been taken that were never going to come to light. Dave Marsh's fair weather friends no longer knew anything.

I should have liked to have spoken to Gelina about this. But we never met again. We saw each other in court, without speaking. Even had we met it is doubtful that she was going to speak freely. She had played her part, and found her revenge. It tasted as revenge always does. It was better not to say anything that might add to the awfulness of it all.

It was as if Dave Marsh had acted alone. The suppliers of women and guns and explosives were never mentioned. They disappeared. They were never traced. Either the trail went cold, or nobody looked too hard. The shutters closed as in a storm.

There were rumours of political involvement. A leading national figure was mentioned. *Private Eye* ran a story about him. He issued a strongly-worded denial through his legal advisors. Tellingly, the leading national figure did not risk a court case over the matter. Nothing more was heard about the matter except by coded allusions that went rounds of the liberal media until the story faded. Everyone knew something. Some people knew a lot. But nobody dared say aloud one truth that might have led to another and another. That process never happened. The general agreement was clear. It was all the fault of Dave Marsh.

The whole thing was presented as his fantasy. Marsh was to pay the price more or less alone. Even he dared not say all he knew. He didn't want to be found hanged in his cell. He wanted to live if only for the impossible hope of establishing his innocence. 'Whatever I did – and I do not regret a thing I did – it was all for my country,' were almost the last words he spoke in court after the sentence was read out.

I told Marsh I had to go. 'I came,' I said, 'because you asked me. I thought you had something to tell me, a word of explanation. I want to hear what prompted you, what made you take such a step, Dave? What happened, Dave? What was the first moment? Tell me.'

'It was something that Simpson said. It set me thinking. When he said I ought to dedicate every day to myself I thought that's right. I thought, I'm going to do just as he says. You see, I believed him. I took him literally. And I thought, Dave, my old son, you go out there and you bloody well get it if you want it. Don't let the buggers stop you. That's what I thought. As I say, I thought like that because of him. I believed him. You should never do that, you know. Never believe what they say. It's all lies. Well, I dare say you know that, being highly educated and that. Well, I have had to survive by my wits. That's how I got on. It was entirely by my own enterprise. Nothing wrong with that, you say, and you'd be right.

'But that's the whole effin' point. I didn't trust to my own judgement. I believed that little bastard. I took him at his word, and I decided to take what was mine. More fool me.'

In the sky there were streaks of golden cloud against the deepening blue. Visiting time was almost over. Very soon I should be driving homeward. Then there was to be the trial, the last time I was going to see any of the people I had known in the garden overlooking the park. A part of my life was about to close, not before time.

'I don't regret it, though,' Marsh said in conclusion. 'I do not regret anything. I nearly saw my dream. It was there just out of reach. But, believe me, it was there. I was prepared to dedicate every day of my life to the vision I saw before me. I was a leader. I was listened to. I had command of the situation. Once you have command you never lose it somehow. I suppose it is destiny. Well, I had command all right. I was winning the war for my country. It was to be my country, a nation that was respectable and respected, a nation where everyone was proud to belong, and everyone knew their place, and they are proud of and glad of it. Those girls were only too willing. Well, that was how I wanted the nation to be – willing, eager, and able. I don't regret that. I don't regret that one bit, not one little bit.'

He didn't rant. He didn't shout or threaten. Marsh spoke so calmly that it seemed that he was rising above everything that was happening. His dream had not faded. He did seem to believe that not only was he innocent, but that he had a right, if not a duty, to talk and act as he did. There he was, a prisoner on remand, accused of many crimes, looking contemplative and serene.

It struck me then for the first time that Dave Marsh was mad. Whether he had been from the beginning it was difficult to say for sure. I had thought him foolish often, and sometimes utterly stupid. But I had never believed him to be mad until that afternoon. Perhaps a certain madness had been there always, waiting for the time to propel him into the abyss. He had lost all reason now. No longer could he see things as they really were. He sincerely believed he was right. And he seriously believed in his own innocence.

Dave Marsh in those final moments reached out his hand to shake mine. It was as if we were old friends meeting again in the ordinary course of life. Nothing serious was happening. It was all a silly misunderstanding that soon would be sorted out satisfactorily.

There would be a party at the house overlooking the beautiful spa town. Fireworks, champagne and laughter would confirm what everyone knew: a new hour was approaching, a new hour with a new man. Our days should be dedicated to that just cause.

'Did you take his hand?' Rissa asked.

'No,' I replied truthfully. 'Do you think I ought to have? I mean, I did know him.'

'You knew another man,' Rissa said. She didn't need to say any more. The door was closed.

Three

The girls from the house next door were watching a spider weave a web out of the dust it gathers. The care it took was so painstaking that I couldn't bear to break it. Cobwebs were a sign of a slovenly house, but it would have been so unfair to the spider and so unkind to the girls to clear the web away as they watched in fascination the spider's work.

There were times in the weeks after the trial when I should break out into a sweat, or I should start to shake for no apparent reason. We could be walking on the shore, or talking of something ordinary like the weather, when the fear overcame me again.

It was fear without reason, fear of nothing in particular. It was fear of everything. It was fear of life in its contingencies and uncertainties. The feeling soon passed. Like a storm, it blew over. I found calm again, especially in our new life. The darkness was unlikely to come again.

'You will trust people again,' Rissa said. 'In time you'll be able to live again as you used to.'

At first, in fact for a long time, I had no faith in therapy. Recalling Simpson, I recoiled from the thought of treatment, as if all therapists were charlatans. In time I came to see that talking to a stranger who was trained to listen began the healing process that I couldn't perform alone. It didn't take too long for me to put to rest the things that continued to haunt me after the events themselves were past, and the people concerned had faded into memory.

Memory, however strong, isn't active feeling. We remember something well, but we don't experience it. Going back to a place we knew, and it looks not at all as we remember it. Old friends return as strangers.

Yet in writing this I have relived the past. I have summoned so much more than memory. Events as they really occurred have come into my life. The smell of wood in the summerhouse where the ear ring was lost: I could sense it again when I re-entered in recollection the summerhouse. And everything else to the crunch of leaves in the park I could feel. I could almost hear out loud voices long since silenced. I could almost touch with my fingers things that I shall never be near again.

The rain began as soon as I walked out into the open air. The prison guard was a tall, heavy man who looked capable of dealing with any recalcitrance. All the guards had that surly look. They were accustomed to dealing with men without the least conscience for their crimes. Their only regret was to have been caught. Dave Marsh was just another number in one among many anonymous cells.

Softer than many, he was to be pitied rather than feared. Like all of them, he was not human the way other people are. He was a wild creature who had to be tamed. The perpetual task of caging these creatures, and then breaking them, hardened the hearts of their overseers. That hardening showed in their faces. The guard who showed me out did not betray the least human feeling to me. I was just another visitor, as nameless as the prisoner I had come to see. My purpose was no concern of the guard's. I should be forgotten the moment the gate was closed again.

I did not exist. None of the events that led to this place had any meaning. Many terrible crimes were contained within those high walls, behind those locked doors. There was nothing special about any of them. They were the acts of sub-human swamp creatures who had no souls.

The rain grew stronger, turning into a storm tempestuous enough for me to take the lesser roads home. On those roads I was able to drive more slowly and with more care. There was less traffic, less hurry. Of course it took much longer to reach home, but it was safer. I felt safer.

I didn't want to be seriously hurt, perhaps even to die, for Dave Marsh's sake. I had a life ahead. It was so good to hear when Rissa whispered to me the news that she was going to have a baby. That had been our plan, delayed by events, but capable now of happening.

I began to feel fulfilled. The new gallery was doing well. Even in the worst of times the rich find ways of investing their money. Restaurants and hotels were opening all along the Dorset coast. A new town was being developed. There was a local fear of a flood of strangers. We shared some of that concern, not of strangers but of over-development. It is easy to destroy the very thing you're searching for, like the people who move into the country away from the city. They bring the city with them in new developments. There were those who argued that everyone had a duty to welcome the business possibilities these new ventures were creating. We were not so sure.

Life changes, not always for the better. But it does move at such a relentless pace. We can never go backward. It's impossible to escape the web once we're caught. Those webs we find in neglected places, they serve as a curiously apt metaphor of the passage of time. And not only a metaphor of time, but of all the contingencies of life: the unexpected visitor, the unexplained disappearance, the unpredictable loss, the equally unpredictable discovery, the lure of curiosity, the power of coincidence, the agonizing choice. We have lived them all, not by choice but by circumstance.

There was that night in the storm, for example, driving home from the prison in the Midlands. Something wholly unexpected happened then. I was somewhere on the border between four counties. There is nothing much at No Man's Heath except the name. There was an inn, closed for repairs, the sign said. Unfamiliar towns were signposted. All were some distance away.

A figure appeared on the roadside in the distance. Approaching, I saw a young woman, soaked in the rain. She had no coat. Her party clothes were a drenched ruin. She looked in deep distress, abandoned by those she knew and lost in the middle of nowhere in the downpour.

Stopping the car, I opened the passenger door. But the woman simply shook her head. She was very pretty and very upset. In a broken accent she said, 'You don't understand.'

'You need help. You look in need of shelter,' I replied.

'No.'

'Please.'

'No.' The woman shook her head defiantly.

There was the roar of an enormous truck coming by. It headlights on full beam flooded my vision so that I could see nothing but light. And when it was past the woman, as in a ghost story, was gone.

I was not hallucinating then. As I say this I am not lying. I couldn't then and cannot now explain what had happened. It did seem very strange, so strange I was reluctant to tell Rissa in case she thought I was deluded.

Rissa did believe me. She thought it strange, of course. Typically she brought some thought to it with her quicksilver mind. Rissa took the event very seriously. She felt it to be a foreboding. The woman was a warning to me to let go of all that was not necessary to the happiness Rissa and I were finding.

And so I wonder what really happened that night. My memory is as I have said. That there was someone by the roadside is not in doubt. The details, though, may have been overlaid with my doubts and fears, with the tempestuous night and the fatigue of the journey. All these factors created something. Not everything happens by chance.

Sometimes we can choose what to make of the world. I see how little the story I've told is about me.

I was there witnessing things, but for most of the time I was on the margins. I had no serious part in any of the things that happened. What involved me was that I came to know the people concerned. They drifted in and out of my life. That was enough to engender a feeling I couldn't break.

Rissa never said to me that those people didn't matter. She knew they did. Her task was to set me free. She took that task upon her because of her love for me.

That love is something rarely to be encountered. At first we find the attraction of beauty and energy and passion. Then there comes the closeness of knowing, a harmony of living. Although life must contain its tensions, that harmony once it is reached is a glimpse of another, higher life. And then there is the gift itself, it was a gift freely given for it to be love.

I felt both so lucky and so unworthy. Such benevolence is rare. It comes only with a selfless acceptance of frailty as well as strength. When we fully love someone it isn't in spite of his or her faults, but because of those weaknesses that seen in someone else should be unacceptable to us. Not only do we forgive those we love, we accept and embrace and receive into our selves those we love.

One night in Andalusia Genevieve was conceived. The day had been hot, as all the days that September were. But the nights were cooler now that the year was waning. Rissa bought a bolero jacket both for style and comfort. It was black velvet that went so well with the matador pants that stressed the roundels of her haunches that crowned those striding legs.

That night I came alive as I had not been alive in a long time. The memories and fears had been vanquished as we moved towards the future of our life together. Soon, as we had planned, our energies would be focussed on another life, the child we had brought into the world in love. Genevieve came later, in her own time. For the moment we thought only of the moment.

In the morning the sun was visible through the shutters. Rissa opened them to let sunlight and air into the room. 'Is this everything you want?' Rissa asked. I whispered something of my hopes for both of us. Rissa smiled and said, 'Of course.'

INDEX

Geoffrey Heptonstall

INDEX

Geoffrey Heptonstall

ISBN 978-1-911424-12-3
SKU/ID 9781911424123

Cover design by Wolf
Book design by Wolf
Editor: Monica Turoni

Publishing Company:
Black Wolf Edition & Publishing Ltd.
2 Glebe Place, Burntisland KY3 0ES, Scotland www.blackwolfedition.com